HOW TO SURVIVE MIDDLE SCHOOL AND MONSTER BOTS

Other books by Ron Bates

How to Make Friends and Monsters

HOW TO SURVIVE MIDDLE SCHOOL AND MONSTER BOTS

BY
**HOWARD
BOWARD**
WITH A
LITTLE HELP FROM
RON BATES

ZONDERKIDZ

How to Survive Middle School and Monster Bots

Copyright © 2014 by Ron Bates

This title is also available as a Zondervan ebook.
Visit www.zondervan.com/ebooks.

Requests for information should be addressed to:

Zonderkidz, 3900 *Sparks Drive SE, Grand Rapids, Michigan 49546*

ISBN 978-0-310-73608-0

Art direction: Cindy Davis
Cover design: Cindy Davis
Illustrator: André Jolicoeur
Interior design: Ben Fetterley and Greg Johnson/Textbook Perfect

Printed in the United States of America

14 15 16 17 18 19 /DCI/ 20 19 18 17 16 15 14 13 12 11 10 9 8 7 6 5 4 3 2 1

Introduction

First, before I say anything else, I want to make one thing clear: some of my best friends are machines. Seriously. There's the clock radio that wakes me up in the morning, the toaster that makes me breakfast, the electric tooth-brush that scrubs my braces, the computer that does my homework, and the night light that's there in case I need to see stuff while I'm asleep.

Machines are totally awesome! Sure, we've had our differences—like that time when I was six and my older brother, Stick, told me our bug zapper was made out of candy. I probably shouldn't have believed him, but he said that's why the bugs kept going in there. It explained everything!

My point is, the second the feeling came back into my tongue, I completely forgave that zapper. I don't even have that nightmare where I'm a moth anymore.

That's why the stuff that happened a few weeks ago seems so unbelievable. I mean, of all people, why me? I'm technology's biggest fan!

You heard about it, right? The trouble at Dolley Madison Middle School? It was all over the Internet—which is why you shouldn't believe it. Once a story like that hits the Web, people add in a lot of gossip and lies and then it spreads like wildfire. So whatever you've heard, forget it.

It's not the real story, because nobody knows the real story but me.

And I haven't told a soul … until now.

Here it is—the good stuff, the bad stuff, and the stuff I was hoping no one would ever find out about. It's time the truth came out. I'll be the first to admit I made a ton of mistakes, and caused a lot of trouble, and put just about everyone I know in danger. So if you feel like you absolutely have to blame someone, then point your finger straight at me. It's my fault.

But just so you know, the robots started it.

CHAPTER 1

The Adventures of Turtle Boy

"Howard ... what are you wearing?"

Mom was standing by the kitchen stove in pink flannel pajama-bottoms and fuzzy blue slippers. She looked at me the way a detective looks at a crime scene.

"Stuff," I said.

I reached across the breakfast table and grabbed the box of Cheerios, then shook it to make sure I wasn't going to pour out a big bowl of dust.

"Yes, I can see that," she said. "But why are you wearing it?"

"Dolley Madison Middle School frowns on nudity," I said.

I sneaked a glance at her over the top of the cereal box. She was rubbing her temples like she does when she's getting a headache.

"Don't do this, Howard. It's too early for one of your stunts."

I loaded up my spoon with a pile of little Os and shoved them into my mouth.

"What's the problem?" I said.

Mom's stare turned into a glare.

"You know what the problem is. You look like … like … like …"

"He looks like a turtle."

A turtle? Who said that? We both turned our heads. There, sitting at the far end of the table, was a sweatshirt that appeared to have swallowed a teenager. Could it be? Why, yes—it was Katie Beth Boward! Imagine that, my seventeen-year-old sister had taken precious seconds away from her iPhone just to call me a reptile. And in her own voice, not a text message!

"Nobody asked you," I said.

"Hey, if you want to be a dork …"

"Stop it," Mom said, stepping between us. "Katie Beth, quit picking on your brother. But, Howard, your sister is right. You look like a turtle."

It was true. I did look like a turtle—and for a good reason. Turtles are awesome! They come naturally equipped with a hard, protective shell they can retreat into at the first sign of trouble. That means they're completely invulnerable to any attack—which, in my humble opinion, is nature's most amazing wonder. And I'm not just saying that as a turtle-loving junior scientist. I'm saying that as a kid who gets beat up a lot.

A turtle shell is every young nerd's dream.

The funny thing is, I wasn't really thinking about

turtles when I started getting dressed that morning. I was just thinking about padding. For reasons I will be happy to explain later, I wanted to make my skinny, pencil-like body as cushy as possible. So I put on an undershirt, covered by a flannel shirt, covered by a lifejacket, covered by a turtleneck sweater. My scrawny legs were crammed into stretchy sweatpants stuffed with a thick layer of Bubble Wrap and cinched with my Sunday belt. But the best part was what went on the outside: a thermal-insulated, water-resistant, arctic explorer-style bubble parka!

You've seen these, right? The puffy ones? The ones that if you try to put your arms down, they spring back up like a jack-in-the-box? The ones made from the same stuff they build bounce castles out of? And when you wear it, you look like a waddling, earthbound version of a balloon in the Thanksgiving Day parade?

Mine is lime green.

"Why would you want to go to school looking like a turtle, Howard?" Mom asked. "You have corduroys hanging in your closet!"

"Corduroy chafes me," I said, and took a giant swig of chocolate milk.

Mom pushed a runaway hair out of her face and looked at me. It was a tired look. And that's when the conversation went where all our conversations eventually go—to the sigh.

"Howard," she sighed, "this is why ..."

She never finished the sentence. She didn't have to. I knew it would have been something like, "This is why you come home with your underwear pulled over your head," or "This is why they laminated your algebra book," because, deep down, that's what everyone really thinks. But everyone is wrong.

The reason I come home with my underwear over my head is because I'm in the seventh grade and the seventh grade is filled with angry, oversized, wedgie-obsessed jerks. I mean, is it my fault I have brains instead of muscles? That my hair looks like a giant cotton swab? That my orthodontia can be seen from space? No. Yet I'm the one who ends up getting noogies and grief. How is that fair? I mean, I don't think my mom was really blaming me. I think she was just being a mom … a mom who firmly believes all of life's problems can be solved with nicer pants.

And maybe grown-up problems can, but not middle-school problems. Because middle-school problems involve bullies, and it's entirely possible for a bully to like what you're wearing and still not like you. They don't even need a reason. Honestly, I can't think of a single thing I've ever done that would cause someone to want to harm me or my underpants—well, except maybe that thing with the monsters. Did I mention there were monsters? Yeah, earlier this semester, I created a mob of large, goo-filled monsters that attacked my classmates and nearly destroyed the school … Popularity-wise, it was not my finest moment. Still, I'm a little surprised things went as badly as they did—maybe the monsters should have been wearing corduroys?

Oh well, live and learn.

As for the laminated algebra book, that was my idea. Neatness counts.

I looked up at Mom and returned her sigh. Was it even worth trying to explain? Probably not.

☆ ☆ ☆

As I told you earlier, I had a reason for dressing myself up like a walking mattress: it was battle armor. I, Howard Boward, was at war. You see, at that very moment, an old enemy was waiting for me just outside our front door—*and his name was winter!*

Winter, as I'm sure you know, is God's way of telling us to stay in the house. Think about it—it's cold, it's gray, there's ice everywhere. I'm just saying there's a reason he gave bears fur and us hot chocolate with mini marshmallows. The evidence against stepping outside is as plain as the nose on your frostbitten face.

But the surest sign God meant winter to be an indoor season is the horrible white menace that attacks us from above: snow, nature's fluffiest weapon!

This year, it was everywhere. Which is why I couldn't believe it when Mom made me lose the lifejacket and the Bubble Wrap and anything else that wasn't technically considered "clothing." It was madness! But for the sake of family harmony, I left them in a sad little pile in the hallway. Then I walked out to face the frozen wilderness alone and defenseless.

Well, not completely defenseless. She let me keep the parka. And when it came right down to it, that was really all I needed. It was huge and plump and weatherproof—an invincible shield against any attack.

I managed to maneuver my way through the neighborhood until I reached the sidewalk in front of dear ol' DMMS—that's Dolley Madison Middle School, for those of you who are unfamiliar. I don't know what your school is like, but mine is a terrifying land of meatloaf and predators. Which is why I paused when I came to the curb—one more step and I'd be in bully country. Quickly, I adjusted my gigantic scarf around my face as a possible defense against attack and tried to yank down my hat as far as it would go. The only parts of my face not covered in some kind of knitted armor were my ears and eyes.

And I still didn't hear or see it coming.

The force of the snowball knocked me flat on my back into a snowdrift, and, like the turtle I so admire, I lay there helpless, my arms and legs pathetically paddling the air. Wet, freezing slush filled both eyes and my favorite nostril. I could hear the sound of laughter nearby—a loud, ugly cackle like a hyena celebrating a kill.

"Oh, epic! Epic! Did you see that? I caught How-weird right in the face!" a familiar voice rang out. "One in a million shot, dude!"

A few seconds later, I could make out two large, blurry figures standing over me. As my vision came back into focus, I saw that one of the blurs had shaggy blond hair and a stupid grin on his face. It was Kyle Stanford. He'd been the thrower, which explained why he looked so happy. Next to him was a pile of muscles and black hair that I instantly recognized as Josh Gutierrez. I wasn't surprised to see them together—bullies often run in pairs. Reaching down, they each grabbed a sleeve of my jacket, and, for a fraction of a second, I actually thought they were going to help me up.

They weren't, of course. Instead, they began pushing my arms up and down in a furious, sweeping motion. When they were finished, they rolled me out of the way and looked down at their handiwork. It was a perfect snow angel. At least it was until Josh pulled off his mitten and used his finger to draw a pair of horns on my outlined head. Then he drew a pointy tail. Finally, next to the indentation, in big, snowy letters, he wrote "HOW-WEIRD WAS HERE!"

"How-weird," if you haven't guessed, is me.

I watched as the two of them slapped their hands together and marched away in triumph. Winter had scored its first knockout of the day.

This morning had gone terribly, terribly wrong. Slowly, I climbed to my feet and stared down at the strange winged image with the spiky horns and the thin, arrow-tipped tail. It was no snow angel—it was a snow devil! Clearly, my turtle powers were no match for this kind of evil.

It was time to admit that if I were going to survive the horrors of winter, I'd need the help of someone so dark hearted, he made Kyle and Josh look like Cub Scouts.

And, unfortunately, I knew just where to find him.

☆ ☆ ☆

A pair of thin, green eyes stared back at me through the crack in the bedroom door.

"Stick," I said, "can I talk to you?"

For those of you who haven't met Stick (and congratulations on that, by the way) he is my fifteen-year-old brother and the source of most of the misery in my world. He eyed me suspiciously and scratched the top of his helmet-like haircut.

"What do you want?" he said.

I gulped.

"I want to be bully-proof," I said. "Can you train me?"

Slowly, Stick's mouth bent upward into a wicked grin. His fingers came together and formed a disturbing triangle in front of his chest.

"I knew this day would come," he said.

CHAPTER 2

G-Force

"Where do you think you're going?" I asked Reynolds Pipkin.

Reynolds is my annoying eleven-year-old neighbor. People think I hang out with him, but I don't. It's more like I'm the sun and Reynolds is a tiny, insignificant planet that orbits around me. I didn't really care where he was going, but I still felt like he should ask permission before breaking away from my gravitational pull.

"I'm going over to G-Force's house," he said.

I raised one of my eyebrows until it was a dangerous-looking spike.

"I want to see his robot," Reynolds explained.

Now, normally, the sight of Reynolds Pipkin leaving is the pleasantest part of my day. But before he could take another step, I moved in front of him.

"Robot?" I asked.

He nodded.

"Forster has a robot?"

He nodded again. "He just finished building it."

"Building it?"

Reynolds looked at me blankly and blinked like an owl. Apparently, my rage breath was fogging his glasses. I showed him my best fake smile and moved out of the way.

"I see. Well, that sounds just dandy, Reynolds," I said calmly. "We'll both go."

☆ ☆ ☆

"Well, look who's here," the red-headed nightmare greeted us when we walked into his yard. "Nice hat, Boward."

I was wearing my wool-knit cap, the one with the ear flaps and moose antlers. I put it on before we left because it makes my brain look bigger.

"Nice mittens, Gerald," I said.

That's right, "G-Force's" real name is Gerald. And he was wearing mittens. And they were nice.

We locked eyes. I've been going to school with Gerald Forster since kindergarten and, for some reason, he's gotten the idea that he's my academic rival. In his dreams!

OK, he has a slight edge on me in English and we're dead even in math. But in science, the only subject that really counts, he's a full 3.4 percentage points behind my average. Three … point … four! The humiliation must be killing him.

"We came to see your robot, G-Force," Reynolds said.

That's another thing—who calls himself G-Force? It's not even a nickname. A nickname is something that someone else forcibly attaches to you, like How-weird or Nerdly McStinkpants. Something you spend hours erasing from the boys' room wall. You don't just get to go around saying "Hi, I'm Gerald, but everyone calls me G-Force," because that's just wrong! Plus, it's a total lie. Everyone does not call him G-Force. And I know that for a fact because *I* do not call him G-Force.

"Yes, let's see it, Gerald," I said.

He hesitated, staring at me out of the corners of those two narrow peepholes he calls eyes. Gerald has freckles and that's fine, but when he scrunches up his face, they all squeeze together into one giant super-freckle. He was scrunching it now.

"Well, I guess it'll be all right," he said. "Just don't touch anything."

"I'll try to restrain myself," I said.

He gave me a smart-alecky look and led us across the yard. When he pushed a button, the garage door rolled back, and I could not believe what I saw.

"Wow," I whispered.

It was clean. You could actually put two whole cars in there! If you'd ever seen our garage, you'd understand my amazement.

Gerald walked over and pulled back a greasy white sheet covering something in the corner. There it was—his masterpiece. It looked a little like a toaster oven on wheels.

"That's a robot?" I asked, somehow managing to hold back outright laughter.

Reynolds scratched his head.

"Maybe that's how they look when they're babies?"

Gerald smirked. It was almost as if he was proud of this embarrassment!

He picked up a silver remote-control box and pushed a small, plastic handle. The toaster went forward. He pushed the handle to the right and the toaster turned right. Then he steered it out into the driveway. We followed.

"Pipkin, hand me that basketball," Gerald said.

Reynolds just blinked.

"It's the orange one," I whispered. Pipkins are not known for their athleticism.

Reynolds grabbed the ball from a bin in the garage, and Gerald took it. Then he pushed another button on the remote control. Suddenly, a long metal arm unfolded from the side of the toaster-bot. On the end of the arm was a bowl that looked kind of like a giant ice-cream scoop. Gerald put the ball in the scoop and steered the robot into position in front of the basketball hoop at the side of the driveway.

"Now watch," he said.

The robot cocked its arm and flung the ball into the air. It went straight through the net. Gerald moved it out farther, and it shot again. It scored again. By the time the demonstration was over, Gerald's robot had made seven out of nine shots.

I couldn't make seven shots if you gave me a ladder.

"Unbelievable!" I gasped.

"Thanks," Gerald said.

Thanks? Wait, had I just given Gerald Forster a compliment? I shook myself out of my robotic daze.

"I meant unbelievable that it didn't get a single rebound," I said.

Gerald frowned, and his super-freckle appeared to be very angry.

"Why did you build a robot anyway, G-Force?" Reynolds asked.

"It's for a contest. I'm in this club, Believer Achievers. They sponsor a lot of science events and stuff."

Wait a minute—there was a group building robots and doing cool science stuff and I wasn't part of it? How could that happen? It was like trying to play chess without your king!

The rectangular robot backed up, pulled forward, and parked itself inside the unnaturally clean garage.

It was a near-flawless performance. My stomach hurt.

"Well, thanks for showing us your little toy, Gerald," I said. "If they decide this contest with a game of H-O-R-S-E, I'm sure you'll do well."

Then I turned around and stomped the three blocks back to our house.

CHAPTER 3

Robot Fever

I couldn't focus at school the next day. My head was filled with little toasters shooting baskets. It was all I could think about. Why had I let Reynolds drag me over to Gerald Forster's house? Now I had the robot fever.

I had it bad.

"Chocolate milk or regular, Howard?" Margaret asked.

Margaret is the nicest lady in the cafeteria and maybe in the whole school. She's sort of like my grandma, except she's bigger and louder and no one likes her food.

"Chocolate, please," I said. "Better make it two."

Margaret looked concerned. "Rough day, hon?"

"Margaret, have you ever wanted something so bad it made you sick?"

"Now, what could you possibly want that bad, Howard?" she asked.

"Gerald Forster's robot."

Margaret put the milk on my tray, then peered down at me.

"Nothing good ever comes from envy. The Bible says it makes the bones rot. You just remember that, hon."

Great. Not only did I not have a robot, my bones were rotting. Gerald was going to pay for this!

I carried my sorrows and chocolate milk to the table with the wobbly leg in the very back of the cafeteria. That's my usual lunch spot. OK, it isn't the most popular location, but at least it was a safe distance away from Ernie Wilkins. Or, as he's better known to the lunch crowd, "Wet Willie Wilkins."

Ernie was a master of the ear assault. From my place at the wobbly table, I'd watch him sneak up behind some unsuspecting kid, put his finger in his mouth until it was good and spitty, and then stick it in their ear. Sometimes he'd get five or six ears before he left the lunch line!

Personally, I've never understood the appeal of the multi-Willie attack. Do you really want to put your finger back in your mouth after it's been in someone's ear? That's just gross. But Ernie didn't seem to mind. Today, he'd hit four victims already, and I saw him stalking a fifth—a new kid named Trevor Duke.

Nobody knew anything about Trevor. Well, except that he was a loner. I don't mean a loner like me—Trevor was a loner by choice. And he looked the part. He was big and wore a leather jacket and had long black hair covering half his face. But mostly the thing that made him a loner was the way he acted. He didn't talk to anybody. Not even the teachers. At least not that I'd seen. Trevor Duke was a mystery.

A mystery who was about to be introduced to Ernie Wilkins' moist, disgusting finger.

But then something freaky happened. Just as Ernie was about to deliver the saliva-stab, Trevor grabbed him by the wrist, twisted his arm, and flipped him onto the ground. It was the coolest kung-fu move I had ever seen by a guy holding a corn dog.

☆ ☆ ☆

My science teacher is Mr. Zaborsky. Personally, I think he looks more like a scientist than a teacher. He's a little short and kind of chunky, with wild brown hair that doesn't quite meet in the middle. Mr. Z calls himself a geek and knows all about inventors, and those are just two of the reasons he is my role model.

Well, not my *main* role model—that would be Benjamin Franklin, the greatest inventor who ever lived. But as far as teachers go, Mr. Z was tops.

"Even if you don't plan on being a scientist," he told the class, "science is still very impor-tant to your future. Each of you is part of the most technologically advanced generation the world has ever known. You're using things right now your parents never dreamed of. What are some examples of technologies you have that previous generations didn't?"

"My phone," Crystal Arrington said.

"Very good. How is it different from the phone your parents had?"

"It's prettier," Crystal said.

Mr. Z smiled.

"Yes, it is," he agreed. "It's a lot prettier. It's also a lot smarter. It takes pictures. It can text. You can play games and watch movies on it. All your parents could do on their phone is talk. And they couldn't even do that unless they stayed home."

"Sounds awful," Crystal said.

"Oh, it was," Mr. Z said. "If it wasn't for the pointy sticks and dinosaurs, we'd have had no fun at all."

The class laughed. Mr. Z scanned the room.

"What else?" he said.

"The Internet," Tammy Kane said.

"Absolutely. The Internet puts an amazing amount of information right at your fingertips. If my generation wanted to know about something, we had to go to the library or, heaven forbid, talk to each other. Anything else?"

"Robots," I said.

"Robots!" Skyler Pritchard yelled from way back in the part of the room I call Slackerland. "You mean like in the movies? He's asking us for real stuff, doofus!"

"OK, first, watch the names," Mr. Z warned him. "And second, robots are real, Skyler. We have robots that build cars and explore other planets. We have robots that perform delicate surgeries. Robots vacuum our floors and water our lawns. There are walking robots and flying robots and robot dogs, and, as we speak, scientists are developing microscopic nanobots so tiny they can be injected into the human bloodstream. There are a lot of jobs people are doing right now that robots can do just as well. And robots don't have to sleep."

"Or eat," I said.

"Well, everything eats, Howard. It's just that instead of a cheeseburger, a robot eats electricity. And if he doesn't get it, he starves just like you and me. But you're right, you don't have to give a robot thirty minutes for a lunch break."

After class, I stopped to talk with Mr. Z.

"This isn't about school. I just wanted to ask if you know anything about a group called Believer Achievers."

"The BAs?" he said. "Yeah, I know a lot about them, Howard. I'm actually one of their science advisors. Were you looking for something specific?"

"No, I just kind of wondered what it's all about."

"Well, let's see," Mr. Z said. "It's a youth science organization, which I'm guessing you already know."

I nodded.

"And you might have heard that there are quite a few kids from this school who are members. I'd say the biggest difference between BA and other science groups is that BA has a faith focus, which means we emphasize things like morality and personal responsibility. Is that the kind of information you were looking for?"

"Well, sort of," I said, digging the toe of my shoe into the carpet.

Mr. Z broke into a broad grin. "And yes, Howard. We build robots."

I looked up and smiled. Mr. Z can read me like a book.

"They're a good group. I think you'd like them," he said. "Right now, we're getting ready for our annual Robotics Fair. If you get the chance, drop by this weekend and I'll show you around."

"I will," I said.

Imagine that—me and Mr. Z hanging out on a Saturday with a bunch of robots. The future was looking brighter already.

CHAPTER 4

Meanwhile, Back at the Lab ...

When I got home that afternoon, I headed straight to my lab and ... Wait, have I told you I have a secret lab? I mean, it's not a huge secret, like Wendell Mullins having a crush on Missi Kilpatrick (don't tell anyone), but I wouldn't want the wrong people knowing about it.

And by the wrong people, I mean my family.

My family has been science-a-phobic ever since they found out that when you mix me with ordinary household products, stuff explodes. I'm not saying they don't trust me, I'm just saying there's a reason they padlock the coffee creamer.

Fortunately, my lab is in a super-secret location: our garage. Or, as I like to call it, the island of misfit junk. Now that's not the same thing as the island of actual junk—actual junk can be thrown away. But misfits are those things that are too good to get rid of but not good enough to actually use. Things like ugly ties; bad school pictures; a canoe that leaks, but only when you put it in the water ... stuff like that. Our garage is literally jam-packed with misfits—at least that's what my family thinks. The truth is, in the very center of the room, surrounded by stacks of cardboard boxes and broken patio furniture, there is an open area suitable for human habitation.

It's my scientific hideaway.

I lifted the garage door, crawled through the abandoned picnic cooler, made a left turn, slithered through the empty filing cabinet, and popped out the door of an old clothes dryer.

When you have a secret entrance, getting there is half the fun.

I flipped on the light. There it was—my laboratory. It's not fancy or anything, but the place has a certain charm. In front of me was my work table and my countertop filled with test tubes and beakers. The hook with my lab coat was in the corner, and up in the rafters was one of those V-shaped metal things that buzzes and makes a spooky electrical arc. It doesn't do anything else, but that's OK. When you look that cool, you don't have to.

But my favorite part of the lab was hanging on the back wall—a picture my dad took of me and Franklin Stine. He's my best friend.

Yep, my little laboratory had everything I needed ... and one thing I didn't.

"Reynolds!" I yelled. "What are you doing in here?"

"Sitting," he said.

"I know that, Reynolds. I can see that you're sitting."

He blinked.

"Then why did you ask?"

I sighed. To be honest, I wasn't all that surprised to find Reynolds Pipkin lurking there in the dark. He has this nocturnal quality. I mean, have you seen Reynolds? He's short and plump, with a pointy nose and thick, round glasses. It's like a wizard granted an owl's wish to become a real boy.

Reynolds has been showing up in my lab uninvited ever since he found the secret entrance. That didn't surprise me either. Reynolds is a snoop, the kind who goes through people's garbage cans, which makes it almost impossible to keep things from him. Anyway, since he already knew about the place, I made him my lab assistant. Then I fired him. Then I hired him again.

Good minions are hard to find.

"I heard there was a fight at your school today," Reynolds said.

"It wasn't a fight," I told him.

"That's not what I heard. I heard Trevor Duke drop-kicked a kid through the cafeteria window."

"No, he didn't!" I said. "Wet Willie Wilkins was coming at him with his spit finger, so Trevor grabbed his arm and flipped him. It wasn't really even a flip, he just sort of rolled him onto the floor. I mean, it was a pretty sweet move, but it wasn't a fight."

"Oh," Reynolds said, sounding disappointed. I'd just

ruined some perfectly good gossip about the mysterious Trevor Duke.

"What do you know about him, anyway?" I asked.

"Trevor? Nothing. Why would I?"

"Because you're the biggest snoop in town. You spy on people."

His owl eyes made two quick blinks.

"I prefer to think of it as data collection," he said.

I shrugged.

"What time is it?"

"Four twenty-eight. Why?"

"I'm expecting a call," I said.

Reaching into my backpack, I pulled out my tablet and punched the power button. A minute later, it beeped at me. A message appeared on the screen. *Are you available for a video chat?*

I connected.

The screen went black and, when it returned, it had a face—a friendly, furry, big-eyed, fang-flashing face.

"Hey, Franklin," I said.

"Hello, Howard," Franklin said. "Are you alone?"

"I wish," I muttered.

Reynolds moved in front of me and pushed his pudgy face frighteningly close to the tablet's camera.

"Hi, Franklin! It's me! Reynolds! Reynolds Pipkin, Howard's neighbor!"

I shoved him out of the way.

"He knows who you are, Reynolds! Get back!"

Franklin smiled. It felt a little like old times. Reynolds

was actually with me the day I created Franklin in the lab. His ball of Wonder Putty turned out to be the secret ingredient in my monster goo.

"Reynolds, don't you have something else to do? Like straightening this place up?"

Reynolds frowned, but he took the hint and walked to the other side of the lab.

"I got your email, Howard," Franklin said. "How is your training with Nathaniel going?"

Oh, I probably should have mentioned that Stick's real name is Nathaniel. I'm the only one who calls him Stick, which is short for Ugly-on-a-Stick, but that's just because other people don't know him as well as I do.

"Yesterday he made me walk back and forth like a duck in a shooting gallery while he nailed me with fudge bombs," I said.

Franklin looked puzzled.

"What's a fudge bomb?"

"It's a snowball with dog doo in the middle," I said. "Until Stick started throwing them at me, I didn't even know there was such a thing."

"He's a good teacher," Franklin said.

"I guess."

"How's everything else?"

I told him about the robot contest, and about the "fight" in the cafeteria, and about Kyle Stanford and Josh Gutierrez turning me into a snow devil. I probably shouldn't have mentioned that last part. Things like that made Franklin sad.

"I'm sorry, Howard. I wish I was there to help you."

"Yeah," I said. "Me too."

I missed Franklin. I mean, we talked all the time, but it wasn't the same since he went away. He had to go—a monster just doesn't belong in the regular world. When

we both figured that out, I uploaded him into Facespace, an Internet site where he could be what he was always supposed to be—a friend. The last time I checked, Franklin had over three thousand Facespace friends, and he seemed really happy being there. But it was a big adjustment, especially for me. I couldn't even bring myself to get rid of the goo that used to be his body. It was just sitting there in a barrel in the ...

Wait a second—where was the barrel? Where was the big silver barrel that always sat in the corner of the lab? I started to panic, but then I saw that Reynolds had dragged it across the room—and was standing on it!

"Get down from there!" I yelled.

I shouldn't have shouted. When Reynolds spun around, the barrel under his feet went one way, and he went the other. Before I could do anything, Reynolds fell onto the floor and, a second later, the big steel barrel toppled over on its side.

KLAAAANG!

My heart skipped.

31

"Don't move!" I said. "Let me check you out and make sure nothing's broken."

"I'm all right," Reynolds said.

"I was talking to the barrel," I growled.

OK, I wasn't really talking to the barrel. But I was definitely talking *about* the barrel. And please don't tell me that my first concern should have been for Reynolds, because I already knew Reynolds was fine. He'd landed mostly on his feet and, besides, Reynolds is eleven. Eleven-year-olds bounce.

But barrels don't. When they hit the ground, they tend to crack and leak. And considering this particular barrel contained a highly experimental, deeply mysterious, extremely unpredictable, mutating, creature-creating substance, that would be a bad thing. I mean, who knew what could happen?

"Haven't I told you never to touch the barrel?"

"I needed something to stand on," Reynolds said.

"It's not a stepladder, Reynolds! It's monster goo! Do you know why we call it monster goo?"

He looked down at his feet, but I just stood there waiting for an answer. It's a little move I learned from my mom.

"Because it turns into monsters," he mumbled.

"Exactly! That's all I'm saying," I said.

Reynolds blinked three times, which I assume in Pipkin language is an apology. Anyway, that's how I took it. I grabbed an end of the barrel and stood it upright. It was lighter than I remembered—unbelievably light. If I hadn't known better, I'd have sworn the goo wasn't in there at all. I wondered what it looked like now, what it felt like. It really was an amazing substance.

"Howard?" Reynolds said, bringing me out of my daze. "Do you want to put it back in the corner?"

I nodded, and together we scooted the barrel back to the forbidden zone.

"Was there something you couldn't reach, Reynolds?" Franklin asked him.

It was a force of habit. Franklin used to be tall, and tall people are always showing off and getting things down from high places. They consider it a superpower.

"I wanted the banana," Reynolds said, pointing to a bright-yellow object on a high shelf above the counter.

Franklin's eyes lit up. He might not have a stomach anymore, but he still got excited whenever someone mentioned food.

"There's a banana?" he said hopefully.

"You can't eat it. It's a dancing banana," I said.

"There's a dancing banana!" Franklin screamed.

Now he was practically frothing at the mouth.

"You've got to see this. It's cool," Reynolds said.

In a flash, he climbed up the cabinet like a chimpanzee, which made me wonder why we had to go through the whole thing with the barrel. When he came down, he was holding my boogie banana. He set it on the lab table.

"Do we have to do this?" I said.

"YES!" the two of them yelled as one.

I shook my head. It's not that I had anything against

the boogie banana, it's just that I'd seen it a million times. The bottom was a black plastic rectangle about four inches wide and, above it, on a springy sort of thing, was this big yellow banana made out of rubber. Glued to the side was a small gold plaque that said "Top Banana," and just below that, in black marker, were the words "In Science."

I'd written that last part on there myself. Sometimes I like to pretend I get awards.

Reynolds grabbed the boom box I keep above the sink and hit the power button. Music blasted from the speakers, and, like magic, the banana began to dance. It bent forward and backward, then shimmied side to side. The faster the beat, the faster it moved. Of course, it wasn't actually dancing, it was just reacting to the sound waves. Still, you had to respect its skills.

When the show was over, I glanced at Franklin's face. It was frozen in the stunned position.

"Wow," he whispered.

What a goober! Franklin thought the dancing banana was some kind of amazing, mystical, magical wonder. I laughed.

Of course, that was before I found out he was right.

CHAPTER 5

Gym Dandy

"All students, please report to the gymnasium for a science assembly."

I pinched myself. Was this a dream? Because in all the years I had been listening to the morning announcements, this was the first time anyone had ever used that particular combination of words: science assembly. My heart was racing! What could it be? A laser show? One of the space shuttles? A lecture on the life of Benjamin Franklin?

I didn't care. All that mattered was that it was about science—which meant, for once, I could sit in the gym without having to give someone a "T" or an "E" or any other pep-related letter. Ooh, unless they were going to have us shout out the periodic table of elements. That would be so awesome! I felt tingly all over and half sprinted down the hall to make sure I got a seat right up front.

As it turned out, rushing wasn't exactly necessary. The gym was practically empty when I arrived, because the rest of the student body was moving at the speed of elderly snails. It was agony waiting for them to fill up the risers behind me. Didn't they know precious science-seconds were slipping away? I bit my bottom lip and tried to relax. Then I saw Mr. Z standing in the middle of the gym next to a tall microphone, and I waved to him. He didn't wave back, but that was cool. Teachers probably aren't allowed to wave to their favorite students, even at a super-wild, totally amazing thrill ride like a science assembly.

"Good morning," he said into the microphone. The feedback from the gym speakers buzzed like a tornado siren, and he took a step backward. "Some of the most exciting work in science today is happening in the field of robotics. We're fortunate to have some very talented young designers right here at Dolley Madison, and one of them has agreed to show us his entry for the upcoming robotics fair. Will you please join me in welcoming G-Force Forster and Basket-bot!"

Basket-bot?

How could they do this to me? How could they build up my hopes and then give me Gerald Forster? It felt like science had walked across the gym floor and punched me in the pancreas.

All I could do is sit and watch as Gerald and his super-freckle walked out to the microphone followed by the small silver toaster on wheels. A few people laughed, and I couldn't blame them. Once you've seen R2-D2, you're pretty much spoiled for any other robot.

"This is Basket-bot, and he, uh, shoots baskets," Gerald said.

And, for the next twenty minutes, that's exactly what Basket-bot did. He hit long shots and short shots and free throws and layups, and every time the ball went through the net, the crowd jumped to their feet and cheered like he'd just won the state championship. Even the UPs were cheering! UPs are our über-populars—they're practically celebrities. I never in my life thought I'd see the UPs clapping for a nerd, but it happened.

And just like that, Dolley Madison Middle School had its first science-superstar … and it wasn't me.

CHAPTER 6

The Call of the Goo

When I got to the lab, I gave the tunnel door a good kick, and it swung open and slammed against the side of the old dryer. The CLANG! was ear bursting.

Reynolds Pipkin didn't flinch. Instead, he just sat there on the metal stool looking out at absolutely nothing. It was like he was playing a video game that only existed inside his head.

I glared at him and walked to my lab table.

"Well?" I demanded.

He put his brain on pause and looked at me. "Well what?"

"Aren't you going to ask me if I had a bad day at school?"

"Is there any other kind?" he said.

This is what bugs me about Reynolds Pipkin—he can be right and still be annoying. I picked up a red shop rag and wiped it across the table.

"Look at that dust! You call this a laboratory?"

"I call it a garage," Reynolds said.

I scowled at him. There is nothing worse than being in

a bad mood and not being able to share it with the people around you. But with Reynolds selfishly refusing to feel miserable, I was forced to take my rage out on dirt. For as long as I can remember, I have been one of those people who cleans when he's upset. There's something oddly satisfying about seeking out unsuspecting scum and destroying it. I clinched the rag tightly in my fist and tried as hard as I could to scrub a hole right through the top of the lab table. When my elbow started to ache, I lifted the rag and inspected my work. The table looked clean.

But it wasn't. It couldn't be. I could still feel an invisible layer of filth, and that's when I knew that the table and the chairs and my beakers and my books and my lab couldn't really be clean, not really, because they were tainted. Everything was.

Just that morning, I had gone to school knowing that I was the undisputed king of the seventh-grade science hill. It wasn't much, but it was mine. Now everything was different. Gerald Forster had pushed me off my throne and I was rolling and rolling, and I didn't think I was ever going to stop.

My eyes darted around the room, desperate for something else to scrub. They locked onto the large metal barrel in the corner. It was irresistibly gross.

I walked cautiously toward it.

"What are you doing?" Reynolds asked me.

"Nothing. Just cleaning."

I pressed the red cloth against the silver metal and rubbed. As I made small, slow swirls with my hand, I had the strangest feeling that I wasn't rubbing a barrel at all—

it was Aladdin's lamp. I half expected a genie to pop out and grant my fondest wish.

"Maybe you should clean something else, Howard," a voice said.

It was Franklin. Reynolds had called him on my tablet.

"I'm cleaning this," I said.

"I know," he said, and I heard worry in his voice. "I just thought you were done with that."

Funny, I thought so too. But now I wasn't sure.

The rag moved to the top of the barrel, and I pressed down firmly against it. Steadily, I moved it around the rim, scrubbing harder and harder, and then I heard a tinny, metal pop.

"Oops," I said.

The lid had opened.

There was a hush in the lab.

"Close the lid, Howard," Franklin said gently.

"OK," I told him.

But I didn't close it. Instead I lifted it and looked down at the forbidden creation inside—my monster goo.

"Do you know how amazing this stuff is?" I said. "Just add the right ingredients and it can become … anything."

I reached down and dipped my hand into the green, gooey slime. It was like touching magic. The secrets of transformation were flowing through my fingers.

"Don't do it, Howard," Franklin said. "It's too dangerous."

I pulled my arm out of the barrel and a big, messy wad came up with it. I'd forgotten how sticky the goo was. Once you picked it up, it was almost impossible to let it go.

"Everything is dangerous," I said, as a slime trail oozed down my forearm. "Like fire. I mean, it can burn a house down, right? But it also keeps us warm and toasts marshmallows and gives off light. You can't just say something is good or bad. It all depends on how you use it."

The last time I'd used the goo, some terrible things happened. I knew that. And still, I couldn't put it down. It was kind of like running into a friend you haven't seen in a long, long time. It didn't matter if you'd had a fight before—that was in the past. Now that you were back together, all you could remember were the good times.

I looked up and saw Franklin staring at me from his little electronic window. He was shaking his head.

"Howard … please don't."

"Will you stop worrying? Look at it," I said, rolling the goo into a harmless round ball. "It's mostly Wonder Putty. What could happen?"

Diving into the barrel with both hands, I pulled out a huge, gelatinous mound and spread it out on my lab table. When I saw it lying there, the memory of my one and only scientific breakthrough came rushing back. I felt this instant surge of power and excitement. Go ahead, let Gerald Forster build a basketball-playing toaster—let him build a hundred! It still wouldn't compare with the spectacular discovery I had on my table at that very moment. This was real science—science that could change lives.

Well, it could change my life, anyway.

"Is it safe, Howard?" Reynolds asked.

41

"Of course it's safe," I said. "I mean, you like Franklin, right? Well, this is the stuff that made Franklin."

"It also made Pookie," Franklin reminded me. "And Mutt and Tarzana and Big Ape and Buffy ..."

"And Steve Evil!" Reynolds gasped. His eyes were the size of bagels.

They were right. The goo had made Steve Evil—"Steevil," as he called himself—and all the other bad monsters. They attacked the school and kidnapped the UPs and came within seconds of hurting Winnie McKinney. And if it hadn't been for Franklin ...

I stopped myself. I didn't like to think about what might have happened if Franklin hadn't shown up when he did.

Still, now that I looked at it lying there all soft and harmless, I realized it hadn't been fair to blame the goo. Because the goo was just a tool, right?

"I really think the problem was the DNA," I said. "I got it from kids like Kyle Stanford and Josh Gutierrez—I mean, looking back, it's so obvious. Bad people turn into bad monsters."

"You know it wasn't just that, Howard," Franklin said.

I ignored that comment.

"I'm not going to make any more monsters, Franklin. What are you so worried about?"

Franklin didn't say anything. But I could tell he wanted to.

"Then what are you going to do with it?" Reynolds asked.

Up until that moment, I honestly didn't know. But then I looked at Reynolds and Franklin, and when I opened my mouth, an answer came out.

"A robot."

"What?" Franklin asked.

"I'm going to make a robot. Look, it's perfect. Robots don't even have DNA. They're machines! All I need is to somehow get the goo to transform into a cool-looking mechanical whatever, and then, the minute I win the contest—ZAP!—I'll get rid of it."

The two faces in front of me looked nervous. So I raised my right hand.

"I, Howard Boward, hereby pledge to use only quality, non-evil ingredients in the making of this robot, and to shut it down if even the slightest thing should go wrong. Does that make you happy?"

Reynolds hesitated but nodded. I glanced at Franklin.

"You know best, Howard," he said. But I don't think he meant it.

"Awesome!" I said. "OK, first things first. What do we want in our robot?"

"Metal? Nuts and bolts?" Reynolds said.

"Exactly. Let's find some."

A quick search of the garage turned up a small jar of nuts and bolts, some loose screws, an assortment of wires, and a couple of aluminum cans. We tossed them into the goo.

"What's next?"

"Electronics," Reynolds said.

This search took longer, but, when we returned to the table, we had a flashlight, parts from an old vacuum cleaner, a burned-out blow dryer, and the remains of a once-awesome TV set. They all went into the goo. Then I added some spare computer components that I kept around the lab for emergencies.

"Anything else?" I asked.

Reynolds thought for a while but couldn't come up with anything.

"Something nice," I heard a quiet voice say.

Good ol' Franklin. He might just be a Facespace friend these days, but he was still trying to protect me from real-world danger. And if it made him feel better to think there was some way we could add a dash of "nice" to our robot mix, well, who was I to argue?

I picked up my boogie banana. It was bright and colorful and fun, and the first time I saw it, it made me laugh out loud. Besides, if real bananas are good for people, I didn't see why a mechanical one wouldn't be good for a robot.

"This is nice, right?" I said, holding it in front of the tablet.

Franklin smiled.

I tossed it into the goo.

"OK, now all I have to do is program it," I said.

Turning on my laptop, I googled "robot designs" and picked an impressive-looking model. And I don't mean one of those weird square robots like Gerald built. I mean the real thing, the kind you see in the movies, the ones with arms and legs and working metal claws that could crush a car. Then I ran a cable from the computer to the goo and stuck the unattached end deep inside the mysterious squish.

"Here goes nothing," I said.

I pressed ENTER.

For the first few minutes, nothing happened. From the look of things, I might as well have connected my laptop to a giant bowl of mashed potatoes. But just when I was about to give up, bubbles appeared on the surface. They grew bigger and took on strange shapes, until the entire concoction on my lab table looked like a boiling goo-stew. The nuts and bolts and wires were gone now, absorbed into the doughy mixture, and it throbbed and vibrated and let out great belches of steam.

I looked at Reynolds. His mouth was wide open like a baby bird waiting to be fed. I tried to smile but realized I couldn't because my mouth was wide open too. This was a glorious sight for scientific eyes!

And then, after the blob had done every amazing thing you could reasonably expect a blob to do, it stopped. I waited for the next fantastic transformation. And waited … and waited … and waited. But it didn't come.

"Is that a robot?" asked Reynolds, squinting through his glasses.

I bit my lip and stepped closer. "No," I said finally. "That's a failure."

The blob on my lab table … was a blob. It had put on quite a show and had grown way too large to put back into the barrel with the rest of the goo. But it wasn't going to walk or talk or do amazing robot stuff. And it wasn't going to beat Gerald Forster. Not unless there was an award for laziest robot blob.

"Get a box, Reynolds," I said.

He looked around the garage and came back with a big brown box that used to hold a dishwasher. On the side were the words "Handle with Care."

I scraped the big wad of useless goo off the table and into the box, then closed the four flaps to seal it inside.

"I'm sorry it didn't work, Howard," Franklin said.

I knew he wasn't really sorry. He was relieved. But it was a nice thing to say.

I headed back into the house and prepared for the next day of school—my first day as the second-smartest kid at Dolley Madison.

CHAPTER 7

Little Den of Horrors

That night, I took a break from my homework and wandered downstairs for a glass of milk. The house was dark except for an eerie blue glow coming from the den. It lured me.

I stepped inside. Our den is a long, narrow room that carries the permanent scent of popcorn and dog shampoo. It's a happy smell. Next to the wall is a big brown recliner, which was laid all the way back, and a pair of white holey tube socks sat on the footrest. I knew those socks. They were part of a package that included sweatpants, root beer, our dogs, and the TV.

"What are you watching?" I said.

"Monster movie," my dad answered.

"What's it about?"

"Monsters," he said.

"Oh."

47

My dad is crazy about monster movies. I bet he's seen every one ever made. Whenever one is showing on late-night TV, you'll find him in the den in those worn-out socks, goofy sweatpants, and an old gray T-shirt that says "Dog Gone? We Can Help." Dad loves dogs. He also catches them. It's his job; he's an animal control specialist.

The TV flickered. There was a giant plant on the screen eating some guy.

"Feed me!" the plant said.

"I've seen this one," I said.

"Me too," Dad said.

"Do you like it?"

"It's OK."

"But it's not your favorite?"

"It's my favorite about man-eating plants," he said.

"Yeah. Mine too."

I reached for the big bowl of popcorn sitting on the end table. Dad bared his teeth at me the way our dog Frisco does when someone tries to take his bone. I pulled back my hand.

"Dad?" I said.

"Yeah, champ?"

"Can I join a club?"

"Sure you can, son," he said. "Don't you give up. One of them will take you."

"No, I mean a specific club. I want to join the Believer Achievers."

"Oh," he said.

We both looked at the TV screen, and that's when I

remembered why the plant was eating people. It was an alien from outer space. Whenever it ate somebody, it would grow bigger, and then later it started sprouting other plants. When there were enough of them, they were going to take over the world.

"It costs forty-five dollars," I said. Mr. Z had given me a flyer that day at school.

"Ask your mother."

"OK. Can I at least say that it's OK with you if it's OK with her?"

He didn't answer. The plant had extended its root-like tentacles and was using them to demolish a building. I couldn't compete with that. Not when Dad was in total monster-mode. His mind had been on monsters for days now, because this weekend was the start of the Mega-Monster Film Festival, a huge annual event where the theaters downtown showed nothing but monster movies. It was a big deal. People came in from all over, and they camped out on the street and dressed up in freaky creature costumes. For Stick and my dad, this was like a second Christmas.

I thought about asking the question again, but decided to quit while I was ahead. Like Dad always says, "If God had wanted us to talk during TV, he wouldn't have invented commercials."

CHAPTER 8

Winnie and the Great Interrupter

When bullies are on the prowl, I find it wise to navigate the hallways as fast as humanly possible. Think of me as a rabbit and the classroom as my safe, protective burrow. But on this particular day, I guess my speed got a little out of control, because I turned the corner and ran—BOOM—square into Winnie McKinney.

"Hey!" she said as pages of her homework floated down on us like giant confetti. "Why don't you watch where you're ... Oh, it's you."

"Winnie!" I said, my voice hitting that high, squeaky level I save for life's most awkward moments. "I'm sorry, I was just ... just ..."

"Forget it, Howard," she said. "I know what you'll say—you didn't mean it."

For a second, I thought she was going to smile—Winnie McKinney has an excellent smile—but she didn't. She used to smile all the time around me, but that was back when we were friends. That had changed for some reason. It might have had something to do with my monsters taking her hostage and trying to make her eat worms.

You know how girls are about worms.

I grabbed a fistful of homework off the floor. "So … how've you been doing?"

She yanked the wad of papers out of my hand and stuffed them into her pink notebook.

"The bell's about to ring, Howard," she said coldly. "I've got to … Did you get into a fight?"

Me? A fight? Anyone who knows me knows I am not a fighter. If anything, I'm a punching bag. I guess I must have looked confused, because she said, "Your eye."

"Oh, that," I said, remembering the bruise from Kyle's snowball a few days ago. "It's nothing. Black and blue are my winter colors."

She took my face in her hands and tilted it toward the light.

"Let me look at it."

"Owwww!" I shrieked.

"Oh, stop being a baby!" It was the nicest thing she'd said to me in weeks. "It's pretty swollen. You better put some ice on it."

"Kyle Stanford already put ice on it," I said. "That's why it's purple."

She let go of my face, and I stood there like an oaf waiting for something to pop out of my mouth. Preferably words. Finally I said, "Listen, Winnie, I know you're mad …"

Before I could say any more, Crystal Arrington, head cheerleader and well-known interrupter of conversations, shoved her way between us. She tossed back her perfect brown hair and dropped a sizeable stack of poster board into Winnie's arms.

"Winnie! I've been looking all over for you! I need you to put up these signs right away. Put them up everywhere—the halls, the cafeteria, the gym. And don't worry about running out—I've got Missi and Joni making more."

"Oh … OK," Winnie said. "What are they for?"

"What are they for?" Crystal asked. She looked stunned. "The formal! The Winter Formal! The biggest event of the semester! What do you think I've been talking about all these weeks?"

I almost said, "Yourself," but thought better of it.

"Anyway," she continued, "we've got tons to do. I'm putting you down for the decorating committee. Also publicity, entertainment, and food."

Lightning quick, Crystal spun around to face me. "You …"

"Howard," I reminded her.

"Whatever. Your job is to keep the nerds away. Plan something geeky for that night like, I don't know, pocket protector lessons."

"Good idea," I said. "Our pockets are dangerously unprotected."

"Awesome," she said, and floated down the hall in search of others on whom to bestow her wisdom.

When I looked back at Winnie, her face was the color of a ripe Gala apple.

"Ooh, she makes me so mad! I wish she wouldn't say things like that," Winnie growled. "You're not really going to tell anyone to stay away, are you?"

"I won't have to. It's a stupid winter formal—just a bunch of people dressing up and dancing. Who'd want to go to that?"

If you've never met Winnie, she's got these green eyes that open up like sunflowers whenever she's surprised. They had just gone to full blossom.

"Oh … right," she said. "Who'd want to go to that?"

I smiled. She smiled. We were bonding over our shared hatred of well-organized stupidity. But even then, I had the uneasy feeling that things were not at all what they seemed.

CHAPTER 9

The Boward Brothers

When I got home that day, I found a note taped to the door.

Howard, don't come in this way. Just cleaned carpits. Come in through the back door. Mom.

Oh, give me a break! I realize I asked Stick to train me, but this was almost insulting! How dumb did he think I was? First, the note was clearly in his handwriting. Second, it specifically said "Howard." Was it all right for everyone else to come through that door, just not me? I don't think so! And if all that weren't bad enough, he misspelled "carpet"—as traps go, this one was too lame for words!

Obviously, he'd be waiting for me, snowball in hand, behind the side gate. Absolutely pathetic ... and just the kind of sneak attack Stick would try. But this time, he'd outsmarted himself. He was the one who was in for a chilly surprise!

I opened the front door and stepped onto a completely dry, not-even-close-to-clean carpet. Did he really think I wouldn't check it out? I headed into the kitchen and stealthily slid back the patio door. This was the moment I'd been waiting for—Stick would never expect me to attack him from behind! I tiptoed out onto the patio.

SPLAT!

Out of the deep blue nowhere, the sky had opened up and dumped a small avalanche on top of my head. Only it wasn't the sky—it was Stick. He was standing on the roof with a trash can full of snow.

"Oh, you are so eeeeasy!" he screamed, laughing so hard I thought for sure he'd do a nosedive off the roof. "Did you see the way I misspelled 'carpet'? That was so you'd figure out it was a fake. And you did! Congratulations on being a total feeb! Consider this another valuable lesson from Nate's school of pain!"

I was fuming. But there was nothing I could do—I'd asked for this! I could still hear the irritating sound of rooftop cackling as I stormed back into the house.

☆ ☆ ☆

When I stepped inside, I ran straight into a snowman. It wasn't a real snowman. It was just a picture in a coloring book. But it was two inches from my nose.

"Yes, yes, I remember," I told Orson, who was expertly steering the picture back and forth to keep it in my view. "I know I promised I'd help you build a snowman."

Orson is my five-year-old brother, and he never asks for anything. He pretty much never says anything. I'll bet I can count on my fingers and toes the number of words Orson has said in his whole life. It's not that he isn't smart—he's like a genius on the computer—it's just that whatever's going on in his brain doesn't seem to want to come out of his mouth. Mom says he'll talk when he's ready. I'm sure she's right.

In the meantime, he finds plenty of other ways to communicate. Like smacking me in the face with a coloring book.

"Will you cut that out!" I said.

Orson was getting impatient because I'd been stalling on the whole snowman thing. Don't get me wrong, I wanted to build a snowman. I just wanted to build it later. Like in July. Because, as I've mentioned, going outside this time of year strikes me as insane—that's where winter lives!

Besides, I had other things on my mind.

"I'm afraid you'll have to wait, Orson," I explained. "I just found out there is this robot contest, and there's a very real chance that my nemesis, Gerald Forster, could win. And what's the point of even having a nemesis if you're going to let him win things?"

Orson lowered his head until all I could see was the top of his brown, bowl-shaped haircut. He might only be five, but he had this guilt thing down to an art.

"All right, all right," I said. "We'll build a ..."

I stopped in mid-sentence and stared out into space. Build? Yes, that's right. You don't *make* a snowman—you *build* a snowman! And I knew someone who could build practically anything.

I walked into the kitchen and dialed the cordless phone.

"Uncle Ben?" I said. "Bring your tools. We're going to build a snowman!"

I looked at Orson and winked. He'd given me an idea and, with a little luck, G-Force and his Basket-bot were in for a very chilly surprise.

CHAPTER
10

The BAs

"Well, Howard, this is what we call the prep floor. It's where the magic happens. I know in class I've taught you that robots aren't magic," Mr. Z said, "but they so are!"

He was in robo-paradise. I laughed. It was weird seeing Mr. Z without a middle school around him, but it was a good kind of weird. For one thing, he got to wear a T-shirt that said "Believer Achievers Robotics Fair." It made him seem less like a teacher and more like an actual person.

Saturday had finally arrived, and I'd taken Mr. Z up on his offer to show me around. We were walking through a great big exhibit hall they use for tractors and stuff during the county fair. All around us were people getting ready for the robot contest. A lot of them looked like they were in high school, but finally we came to a group about my age. We stopped at their work area—and that's when I saw him.

"Howard, you know G-Force," Mr. Z said.

Gerald was sitting at a long workbench surrounded by

dozens of tiny mechanical parts. We looked at each other like two Siamese fighting fish sharing the same bowl.

"I think you'll be surprised by his entry this year. It's a real contender," Mr. Z said. "Especially if the judges are hoops fans!"

Gerald grinned. It was the kind of stupid grin Stick gets when he scores a hockey goal or someone asks if he's growing a mustache.

Mr. Z must have forgotten about the science assembly. "I've seen it," I yawned.

Gerald was working with another kid, Richard Patel. He was about our age and had a wide, friendly smile and short, shiny black hair.

"Oh, so you've got a partner!" I told Gerald gleefully. "How interesting! And here I was thinking you built that robot all by yourself."

Gerald rolled his eyes and went back to work.

"No, he built it," Mr. Z said. "Everyone builds their own entry. We've got adult mentors who give technical assistance, of course, but the kids do the work. Richard's just helping him make sure everything is in top shape for the contest."

Wait a minute ... helping him?

"Aren't you in the contest?" I asked Richard.

"Yes, this one over here is mine," he said.

He picked up a remote control and summoned a small robot rolling on what looked like the wheels of a toy tank. On top of it were a series of rods and gears—and a golf club.

"I call it Putt-Putt," he said.

"That plays golf?" I said.

"Well, it doesn't have the accuracy of Basket-bot, but, yes. It can sink a putt."

"What are these?" I said, pointing to a patch of dark, shiny squares.

"Those are solar cells. They absorb sunlight and help recharge the battery. It was G-Force's idea."

Now I was really confused. I looked at Gerald, then back at Richard.

"But don't you want to beat … G-Force?" I asked him.

"I'm *going* to beat him," Richard said, smiling.

Gerald pushed him on the shoulder.

"Then why are you helping him?"

Mr. Z grinned.

"We have a little different philosophy here, Howard," he said. "Yes, everybody wants to win, but we also support each other. We all learn from each other. That's why we're here—to connect with people like us and share what we know. I mean, if someone just kept everything to himself, what would that get him?"

"First prize?" I said.

Mr. Z must have thought I was joking, because he laughed.

"The BAs are about a lot more than collecting trophies, Howard. Don't worry, you'll learn."

☆ ☆ ☆

I spent the next hour meeting other contestants and seeing their projects. Some of them were really good. My personal favorite was the Butler-bot, which was built by an eighth-grader named Jennifer Cruz. Basically, it looked like a ventriloquist dummy riding a skateboard. The little man was wearing a tuxedo and had a permanent smile on his face. In one hand, he carried a large silver tray, and by rolling along on his wheels, he could deliver food to a table. He could also turn his head, wink his eye, and fill a glass with water.

He was awesome!

Lots of them were awesome. There were window-washing robots, and robots that could walk your dog, and dog robots that could walk humans. This was the best club ever!

When it was time to break for lunch, everyone came together in a circle and joined hands. We bowed our heads and gave thanks for the food and the group, and I silently gave thanks that I wasn't standing next to Gerald Forster.

Nothing can ruin a good day faster than having to hold hands with your nemesis.

"So, how do you like it?" Mr. Z asked.

"This place is great!"

"I'm glad to hear you say that," he said, "because next year, I want to see your entry out here on the floor."

"Oh, you won't have to wait until next year," I told him.

"What do you mean?"

"I mean you'll see it this year."

Mr. Z looked confused.

"Howard, the contest is in nine days. These guys have spent months getting their entries ready. I mean, you've seen their robots—you can't do something like that overnight."

He was right, I couldn't do it overnight. It had taken three nights. I probably could've done it in two, but Uncle Ben had a little trouble finding some of the parts. You've got to expect delays when you're dealing with advanced technology.

"Oh, I think I can come up with something cool," I said.

In fact, I was pretty sure it was going to be the "coolest" robot in the whole contest.

CHAPTER 11

The Snowbot

When I got back to the house, I found four figures waiting in my yard: Orson, my dad, Uncle Ben, and a snowman.

The snowman was the only one smiling.

"What is this, Howard?" Dad asked. Orson must have just pulled him outside.

"A snowman."

"Haven't you forgotten something?"

"Like what?"

"Oh, I don't know … snow?" Dad said.

OK, I'd made a few modifications to the traditional snowman design. The first one was getting rid of the snow. It's an unstable building material, and it made my hands cold. So instead, I used a plastic snowman that our family puts in front of the house at Christmastime.

I didn't see what the big deal was. Everyone loved that snowman.

"Well, you see …" I started.

My dad stopped me.

"Howard ... what happened to his arms?"

"What?"

"His arms."

"Oh. I cut those off," I said.

Let me explain: His arms were in the way. So I hacked them off and replaced them with a pair of holes so that his new robotic, metal arms could stick out and grab stuff. And I have to say, they looked fantastic!

But not to everybody.

"You cut off his arms?" Dad yelled. "What were you thinking?"

Actually, I was thinking this was a pretty great idea. I mean, Orson wanted a snowman, I wanted a robot—we got a snowbot. It was the best of both worlds. The tall, plastic body slid right down over the motorized frame and covered up all the awesome robotic stuff Uncle Ben brought over from his shop.

"Relax, Johnny," Uncle Ben said, which is what he always said when Dad's face reached a certain shade of red. "It's not as complicated as it looks. Basically, it's like one of those little remote-control cars. Only instead of a car, we used a riding mower."

"My riding mower?" Dad howled.

"We'll have it put back together by spring," I promised.

Dad puffed out his cheeks like a balloon and slowly blew the air out between his lips. It's not a pretty sound.

"Howard," he said, taking off his ball cap and running his hand through a mop of messy black and gray hair, "I know you like to tinker around with stuff like this. But you made a promise to your little brother. All he wanted was to come out and build a snowman with a corncob pipe and buttons for eyes. That's all. And you went and turned it into some kind of ... Power Ranger."

For the record, my dad thinks the Power Rangers are robots.

"But you haven't even seen how it works yet," I pleaded. "Give it a chance!"

To be honest, I thought it was over. Dad looked irritated beyond the point of no return. For several seconds, he just stood there letting his fatherly heat vision burn deep into my skull. But finally he said, "All right, let's see it. Orson, go get your mother."

Dad likes to have Mom there whenever I unveil one of my experiments. She knows where the fire extinguisher is.

All right! I was going to get to do a demonstration! Not to brag, but demonstrations are kind of where I shine. I mean, it's not enough that the snowbot looked awesome. If it was going to win the robot contest, it had to do awesome things. And, in this case, that meant rolling forward, extending its arms, and giving the judges a hug.

That's right, a cuddly, gliding, metal-armed snow-hugger ... Beat that, G-Force! If the judges survived, that trophy was as good as mine.

It was a perfect plan—I knew it the second it popped into my head. The only problem was that I had no idea how to build a robot. That's why I had to call in Uncle Ben. Not only is he the coolest uncle in the world, but he's an amazing electrician. And talk about smart! He can go on for hours about computers or advanced technology or how space warlords are plotting to overthrow our planet. A lot of the stuff he knows, they don't even teach us in school! And besides, if a thirty-six-year-old techie who loves comics books and sci-fi can't help you build a judge-hugging electro-snowman, who can?

Orson rushed back out of the house, dragging my mom behind him. She must have thought it was an emergency, because she was wearing mismatched gloves and the light-up reindeer sweater she'd banned from all holiday photos. Her eyes instantly locked onto the happy, plastic, soon-to-be prize-winner in the front yard.

"Is that Mr. Jolly?" she asked, referring to his former life as a lawn ornament. "What happened to his arms?"

"Don't ask," Dad muttered.

"Now everybody stand back," I said, an unnecessary warning if ever there was one, "and prepare to be dazzled!"

I pushed the snowbot onto the driveway and whipped out the remote control Uncle Ben had made for me. This baby was high-tech! Holding my breath, I pushed the power button to activate the motor. It started! Then, very slowly, Mr. Jolly began to creep forward on his knobby, rubber wheels. At the same time, he raised his arms into their fully extended, hug-ready position. It was working! It was working!

"Well, I'll be," Dad said.

I looked back down at the remote and pushed an arrow. The snowbot turned right. Instinctively, Mom stepped in front of Orson to form a human shield. I laughed. Then I pushed the other arrow. The snowbot turned left. This was one sweet mechanical snowman! I pushed the UP arrow. It picked up speed. I pushed the DOWN arrow. It picked up more speed.

I pushed the STOP button. It went into overdrive! Now it was really moving, which is why Katie Beth could not have picked a worse time to come out of the house.

Frantically, I tapped the OFF button. Nothing! I tried to warn my sister, but, as usual, a pair of headphones was blocking her ears. By the time she looked up, he was practically on top of her.

"AIGGGGGGH!" she screamed, and made a wild, terrified dash through the yard.

If I hadn't known better, I'd have sworn that Mr. Jolly was chasing her. He seemed to match her every turn.

"Katie Beth!" I yelled. "Don't let him hug you!"

The prospect of a robot hug appeared to be too much for her to handle, and she dove headfirst into our euonymus hedge. The snowbot paid no attention, rolling right past her and out into the street.

"I'll stop it!" I said.

Now the thing about snowmen, even plastic ones, is that they're really good on ice. I, on the other hand, am not. Every time I'd start to close the gap, he'd turn a corner and send me belly-sliding through the intersection. At one point, I thought he'd lost me, but then I saw Mrs. Gilroy standing in her driveway. She'd dropped two bags of groceries on the ground and looked like she might be in a mild state of shock. She was staring due north.

"Good afternoon, Mrs. Gilroy," I said, and headed in the direction of her gaze.

It wasn't long before I caught sight of him again. He'd wheeled onto a side street, and it looked like our chase might finally be coming to an end. He still had me by a half block or so, but I was closing fast. And that's when I noticed this street looked kind of familiar. Very familiar, actually. The past few blocks had been a blur, but I suddenly realized I now knew exactly where I was. I was on Mulberry Street.

I gulped.

I WAS ON MULBERRY STREET!

I was chasing a runaway lawn ornament down the middle of Mulberry Street—or as it's known to every kid in town, Snowblind Alley. The seriousness of the situation hit me about the same time as the first snowball.

After that, it was an onslaught. Snowballs flew from everywhere. They came from bushes and from behind trees. They rained down from the sky. I tried to dodge, but there were too many. Within thirty seconds, every single inch of my body had been pelted.

This was my punishment for breaking the neighborhood's first law of survival: don't go down Mulberry Street. Snowblind Alley is winter's icy heart. This is the place where the toughest, meanest, orneriest, most hate-filled bullies in Dolley Madison gather for their snow wars. And when they get tired of pummeling each other, they bombard passing cars or mail trucks or garbage men or stray dogs—basically anything that moves.

And if some poor, unsuspecting nerd should happen to make a wrong turn on his way to the library—Lord help him!

I tried to surrender, but every time I opened my mouth, a projectile landed in it. Not all of them were snowballs. When I finally made my way back to the corner, I turned just in time to see the snowbot gliding across an open field.

As I stood there watching him slowly fade into the distance, I wondered if I might someday hear stories about his fascinating adventures in faraway lands.

☆ ☆ ☆

By the time I got back to the house, the yard was empty and Dad's truck was gone. Apparently, he and Uncle Ben had joined the chase on wheels. Good. Maybe they'd find

Mr. Jolly; not that it mattered anymore. The dream—my dream—was over.

I walked into the house and pulled my battered, snow-covered body up the stairs. Getting out of my wet, dripping things, I stepped into the shower and set the water to steaming. Gradually, my skin lost its blueness, and I began to feel human again. When I was fully defrosted, I stepped out, dried myself thoroughly, and slipped into my warm terry cloth robe. This was the way to spend a winter. Inside. Away from danger. I'd been foolish to attempt to build a robot that lived outdoors. I realized that now.

I strolled down the hall until I was back in my own room. It felt good there. It felt safe. Time to get dressed and get on with the rest of my life—my *indoor* life. I remembered Mom saying something about corduroys hanging in my closet. Now that I thought about it, there was nothing wrong with corduroys. Not really. They were a nice, reliable, indoor trouser. I opened the closet door.

WHAP!

A cold, mushy slushball splattered against my chest.

"Today's lesson," Stick said from behind the coat hangers, "is always expect the unexpected."

CHAPTER 12

A Math Problem

On Monday morning, I dragged my visibly bruised body to Mr. Z's room and told him I had to quit the contest because my robot ran away.

"Ran away?" he said.

I nodded.

"All by itself?"

I nodded again. Mr. Z gave me a weird look. I think he thought I might have a severe head injury.

"Howard … would you like to go talk to the nurse?"

"Why? Has she seen Mr. Jolly?" I said.

"What?"

"Never mind."

It didn't matter. There were only six days until the robot contest. Six days until Gerald Forster picked up his trophy.

"All right, class," Mrs. Washington, my algebra teacher, said. "Pair up, because you're going to be working with a partner for the rest of the period."

Partner? No! Was she serious? Nothing stirs dread in the heart of the American nerd more than the word "partner." I watched helplessly as desks squeaked and crashed and spun around like bumper cars, until there were only two remaining unpaired students.

"Howard, you're with Trevor," Mrs. Washington said.

Oh, great. My partner was Trevor Duke, the silent knight. It all made sense now. Obviously, Mrs. Washington's plan was to partner the smartest kid in class, which was me, with the kid who hadn't answered a single question all semester. It was pretty clear who'd be carrying the load on this one. I stared back over my shoulder at the desk sitting in the deepest, dumbest part of Slackerland.

There was Trevor ... slacking. Or whatever it is that slackers do. His legs were stretched out in front of him like the desk was some kind of a recliner, and he was scribbling on his notebook. I waited. He didn't move. Big surprise—I guess moving was going to be my responsibility too! I scooted my desk across the floor with my feet until we were sitting face to face.

"Hi," I said. "I'm Howard Boward. I, uh, sit over there. Usually."

If he noticed I was in front of him—or even in the room—he didn't let it show.

Mrs. Washington wrote an equation on the board and

gave each team the last ten minutes of class to come up with the answer. It was a tough one, all right, but I thought I could handle it. The hard part would be making it look like Trevor helped.

I sat there thinking about it for a few minutes, then got up to sharpen my pencil. It was pretty sharp already, but the awkward silence was killing me. I took my time, staring out the window and pretending my pencil was really, really, really dull. But just when I was about to head back to my desk, I noticed something moving outside. Two figures wearing cheerleader jackets were carrying something under their arms. When they turned around, I could see it was Crystal Arrington and Missi Kilpatrick. They walked out to an area in front of the school and began unfurling a long white sign attached to two poles.

"Register Now for the Dolley Madison Winter Formal," it said. The letters were made entirely of purple glitter.

What was going on? Was this supposed to be educational? Were teachers letting cheerleaders out of class now just so they could put up big, stupid signs?

I went back to my desk and sat down.

"Some sign, huh?" I said to Trevor.

For the first time, he put down his notebook, took a long, hard look out the window, and then glanced at me. He seemed puzzled. I guess not everyone is as concerned about excessive glitter use as I am. Then he went back to his doodling.

I shifted my eyes back to the window. The sign was still there, but Crystal and Missi were gone. Unfortunately, so were my ten minutes.

Oh no! While I'd been staring at that ridiculous sign, the clock had been ticking. This was terrible! I had nothing on the page! I hadn't gotten the answer! I hadn't shown my work! Me! Howard Boward—the boy who once started a petition to have mathletics declared an official team sport—would get a zero for the day!

The bell rang. I turned to Trevor with a look of horror and apology on my face. But he gave no indication that it mattered to him one way or the other. Instead, he rose from his desk, grabbed his backpack, and headed for the door.

As he passed, he handed me his doodle sheet.

It was the equation—the one on the board. He'd solved it! And correctly, from the looks of things. Suddenly, I realized there was a whole new side to the mysterious Trevor Duke: loner, rebel, math whiz.

CHAPTER 13

Prombies

I was still pretty confused over what happened with Trevor when I spotted Winnie McKinney in the hall. She was walking with Gerald Forster.

Naturally, I felt it was my duty to rescue her.

"Hey, Winnie!" I said with as much enthusiasm as I could fake. "Gerald," I murmured.

Winnie threw me a courtesy glance.

"Do you need something?" she asked. She looked like she was warm enough in her pink sweater and fuzzy white boots, but her voice had an unmistakable chill.

"Nope. Just thought I'd come over and see what's up. Sooooo ..." My eyes shot to Gerald and my voice deepened to tough-guy level. "What's up?"

"G-Force said he'd help me get things ready for the winter formal," Winnie said. "Someone's got to set up the lights and the speakers, and, well, he's kind of a genius with electronics."

Gerald's grin was so cheesy, it almost made me lactose intolerant.

"Of course, I thought about asking you, Howard, but then I remembered what you said. You know—that formals are stupid. Isn't that what you said?"

"Ummmmm," I ummed.

"So, obviously, anyone who wanted to go to the formal would have to be an idiot, right? And I couldn't ask you to waste your time on a bunch of idiots."

Winnie was acting weird. She didn't really sound angry, it was more like she was ... hurt. What had I done? Quickly, I shifted to Plan B: continuous babbling.

"Well, you see, the thing is, when I said that, I ..."

Plan B was getting me nowhere. It didn't matter, though, because at that very instant, Joni Jackson, a girl with a jet-black ponytail and four earrings in each ear, came sprinting down the hall. She was screaming, "Napkins! We have napkins!"

And she'd brought proof. In her grip was a small purple paper square that she waved like a flag on the Fourth of July. I turned my attention back to Winnie. She was gone. Looking around, I saw a huddle of about ten or so girls who'd gathered to celebrate the glorious arrival of something you wipe your mouth with.

I was dumbfounded. Wendell Mullins stopped and stood next to me.

"Weird, huh?" he said.

"Yeah," I answered. "What's going on?"

"Prombies," he said.

"What?"

"They're prombies. It happened to my sister a couple of years ago just before the senior prom. One day she was just a regular person, the next day all she cared about was dresses and shoes and long, sparkly streamers. It's the prom. It makes them lose all will of their own."

"But this is middle school," I said. "We don't even have a prom!"

Gerald shrugged.

"Proms. Formals. Socials. Weddings. They're all the same. If you've got fruit punch and a guestbook, you're gonna have prombies."

I looked at Wendell. He was a scrawny kid, a full head shorter than me, but his voice was as deep as a bullfrog's. So when he told you something, you tended to believe it—mainly because he sounded like a TV newsman.

But Prombies? Nah ... Not at our school. I knew these people. Then I saw the mob in the middle of the hall squeezing closer together, lured to the glorious napkin. And, just like that, I knew.

They were feeding! They were feeding on fanciness!

It all made sense now—the glazed eyes, the pack mentality, the bizarre hostility toward us "normals." I'd seen enough monster movies to recognize the symptoms. Wendell was right!

"It's an infestation!" I shrieked. "We've got to warn Winnie!"

I started to move, but Wendell grabbed my arm. He pointed to the crowd.

There was Winnie McKinney. She was performing a strange ritual that involved holding her hair in a twisted ball on top of her head. Apparently, she could not put it down again until she'd answered a series of questions about what earrings she'd be wearing. I felt my knees go weak.

Wendell put a hand on my shoulder.

"Too late," he said. "She's one of them now."

CHAPTER 14

The Forbidden Box

"It was weird," I told Franklin when I got to the lab. "One minute I'm talking to Winnie, and she seems kind of mad at me, and the next minute she's laughing and squealing with a bunch of girls."

"Maybe it's cooties?" he said.

I don't know where Franklin got the idea that girls have cooties. Unless it was something I accidentally told him during one of my monster education lectures. Probably the one I call "Why We Never Go into the Girls' Bathroom."

"Who knows?" I said. "Anyway, Wendell says everything will be all right when the Winter Formal is over. You want to hang out with me while I study?"

"Sure," Franklin said.

I reached for my backpack, which was sitting on the counter. I guess I must have bumped the backpack against the switch on my boom box because, all of a sudden, music blasted out of the speakers. I reached for the OFF switch.

"Hey, don't turn it off!" Franklin said. "I like that song."

I looked at the tablet. Franklin's eyes were closed, and he had a goofy expression on his face. Then he raised his hands above his head and began to rock out to the ear-splitting sound of the beat.

"Are you finished? I've got to study!" I yelled over the noise.

"What?" Franklin said.

I reached over and turned down the volume to a level where at least the walls weren't shaking.

"I've got to study!" I repeated.

"OK," Franklin said. "After this song!"

It was a long song. But it was a good song, and, after a minute, I found myself bobbing my head. Then I bobbed my whole body. Before I knew it, I was swinging my arms and kicking my feet.

"What are you doing, Howard?" Franklin yelled.

"Dancing!" I yelled back.

"You're kidding."

This is why I only like to dance when I'm by myself. Nobody appreciates my sweet, unconventional moves.

"What if I added some ninja kicks?" I yelled.

"Ninja kicks do make everything better," Franklin said.

I was just about to insert them into my routine when, suddenly, I froze.

"What is it, Howard?" Franklin asked.

Carefully, I picked up the tablet and turned it until it faced the far corner of the lab. The box—the one I'd put the robot-goo into—was moving!

"Why is it doing that, Howard?"

"I don't know," I said.

I pressed the OFF switch on my boom box. The music stopped—and so did the box.

I turned it on again. The box began to bounce.

"Whoa!" I said.

I walked slowly to the big, bouncing cardboard box and opened it. There inside was the living goo, pulsating and vibrating to the sound of the music—just like my boogie banana used to do! The goo had expanded, and now the box was in danger of overflowing. A rush of excitement came over me, and I laughed hard and loud like a mad man.

No ... I laughed like a mad *scientist!*

"What's going on, Howard?" Franklin said.

"It's the goo," I told him. "It's dancing!"

Franklin didn't share my excitement. In fact, he looked horrified.

"Stay away from it, Howard! You know what it can do."

Franklin was a born worrier. Clearly, he was going to let himself get all worked up over this, and I didn't have the time to deal with it. There was so much to do.

"Relax, I'll take care of it. But it was great talking to you, buddy. I'll tell you all about it later," I said.

"Wait, Howard—the goo!" Franklin protested.

His words came too late. I touched the screen and disconnected.

☆ ☆ ☆

I rushed to the box and looked in on the fantastic slime. The experiment had worked! I mean, the blob still looked

like a blob and all, but at least it was doing *something*.
Quickly, I scanned the garage for materials that could help
me take the project to the next level. Because if the goo
was going to become a robot, it needed to look like a robot.

Well … sort of like a robot.

The big square box it was in at the moment worked
fine for a body. I came across a smaller box filled with old
birthday cards and emptied it. That should take care of
the head.

The arms were easy—dryer hoses. You know, those
flexible vent hoses that attach to the back of a clothes
dryer? The ones that look like giant silver earthworms?
There were lots of them lying around the garage, and I
chose two that seemed to be in the best shape. For hands, I
used rubber gloves.

His legs were another matter because they'd have to
hold his weight. I found some PVC pipe that looked good
and sturdy. I figured those should work.

And finally, for his feet, I grabbed a couple of plastic dog
food bowls that our dogs, Frisco and Pants, weren't using
anymore. Perfect!

Now it was just a matter of putting the pieces together.

☆ ☆ ☆

A few hours and a lot of glue later, I was finished. The
robot was complete!

Well, as complete as a robot can be when he's made
out of cardboard, aluminum foil, and duct tape. I'll admit

he wasn't one of those flashy robots like you see in the movies. And he didn't have booster rockets, or heat vision, or that death ray I'd set my heart on. But that didn't mean he wasn't totally awesome. I'd added some finishing touches to make him look more like a high-tech machine and less like a pile of dirty brown boxes. For instance, his torso now had switches and knobs, and I used parts from an old TV to add a cool antenna and wiring from his body to his head.

On his face, I'd glued two electrical plugs where his eyes should be, and I'd cut a slit for his mouth and installed a coil for his mouth that could adjust from a smile to a frown.

He was magnificent! Did he look like the sleek metal design I'd pulled up on my computer? No. But he looked a lot more like a robot than Gerald's Basket-bot.

Besides, the Robotics Fair wasn't a beauty contest. What mattered was what the robot could do. Which was a problem because, at the moment, all it could do was bounce up and down to loud music. That was pretty cool, but probably not good enough to win. When I'd created the monsters, I discovered the goo had this incredible ability to absorb information. It just made things work. So I was counting on it doing the same thing for my new friend. I reattached the cable from my laptop, uploaded some basic commands, and held my breath.

It was time to test it.

"Robot," I said in a loud, commanding voice, "take one step forward!"

Then I waited. I could feel my palms sweating, and my heart was beating so fast, I was surprised it didn't explode. But, slowly, one of the PVC pipes began to quiver and then—he stepped!

He stepped! Somehow, don't ask me how, the goo had expanded itself until it filled both of the robotic legs.

"Robot, raise your right arm," I commanded.

He did it! Do you know what that meant? It meant that the goo had filled the robot's arms! And also that he knew the difference between his right and his left! Which meant he was already at least as smart as Stick.

I was overjoyed! I had an actual, functioning robot that could walk and raise its arms and … what else could it do?

I had to know.

"Robot, follow me."

I marched around the lab in a small, quick circle, and the robot stayed in my steps. So I made another circle. He did it again. It was amazing! Excitement bubbled up inside me like a boiling volcano of happiness. But to find out what he was really capable of, I'd need more space—and that meant going outside. Checking my watch, I saw that it was late; my family would be in bed by now. Even better, the darkness would give me cover from the prying eyes of our neighbors. I decided to risk it. Slowly, I opened the dryer door and crawled into the tunnel. Then I waited.

A few seconds later, the robot's square head entered the tunnel. Unfortunately, that's as far as he got. It hadn't occurred to me that a dishwasher-sized box was too big and bulky to slip through the round, narrow tunnel. Now I had a robot clogging the exit like a cork stuck in a bottle.

"Robot. Go back!" I said, pushing against the top of his head with both my feet.

The robot stumbled backward, and I climbed out of the tunnel.

Obviously, I had a problem. And since I couldn't make the tunnel bigger, there was only one solution—a second way out. Working quickly, I removed pieces from the wall of the clutter between my lab and the garage door until I had a perfectly formed, robot-shaped hole leading to the outside world.

"There you go," I said, "your own robot doggie-door. Give it a try."

The robot hesitated for a minute, examining the opening carefully. I didn't blame him. If I'd just had my head stuck in a dryer, I'd probably be nervous about unexplored holes too. But, at last, he moved forward and passed through the opening. We'd made it to the great outdoors!

I led my new creation out into the yard and had him walk around and grab tree branches and lift an old bucket. I didn't know if he was having fun, but I was having a blast. I had a robot—one that would do anything I told him!

Suddenly, I got an idea: a crazy, wonderful idea.

"Wait here," I told him.

I ran back to the lab, and when I came out again, I was carrying my boom box.

"OK, robot. Have you still got the bounce?" I said.

I turned the volume down to a whisper and pressed the ON button. The music started.

"Bomp. Bomp. Bomp. Bomp," came out of the speakers.

When the quiet beat reached the goo-man, he didn't bounce like he had when he was just a box. But I was pretty sure I saw him sway. It wasn't much, but it was enough to give me hope. I changed the music to something peppy and nudged up the volume.

Now the sway turned into a full-fledged wiggle. I bit my lip to keep from squealing, and also to see if I could still feel my face. Because, in the excitement, I'd forgotten that it was freezing outside. For once, I didn't care. I had a robot. A dancing robot! And that was cooler than anything winter could throw at me.

I had to see more. Forgetting about how late it was, I cranked up the boom box. And then … WOW!

"BOMP! BOMP! BOMP! BOMP! BOMP!"

The vibrations seemed to pulsate through the robot's entire body. His head bobbed. His arms stretched out. Suddenly, it was like he wasn't made out of boxes at all. He was some kind of liquid cardboard, a mound of giant brown Jell-O cubes jiggling to the beat.

I turned the knob, and the music got louder. The speakers boomed, and the robot shook and rocked and shimmied. I was ecstatic! And it wasn't just because I thought I was going to win some robot contest. It was because Gerald Forster was going to lose.

This was a great day for science!

Spontaneously, I broke into a dance of my own. Well, it was what I called a dance. Have you ever seen a hooked swordfish leaping out of the water to try and shake loose from a line? It was like that, only with ninja kicks.

Triumphantly, I swung my hips and pumped my fists and strutted around the yard. The music was pounding, and the robot was groovin', and my mom was on the porch and ... my mom was on the porch!

What was she doing out here? She had on her pink robe and flannel pajamas, so there was a pretty good chance she wasn't out for a moonlight stroll. I froze in mid-gyration.

"Howard," she said, her voice a mix of aggravation and confusion. "What are you doing?"

"Ummmm ... dancing," I told her.

"Dancing?" she said. "In the front yard? At night? With a robot?"

I was wondering when she was going to bring up the robot. I mean, you'd think a bunch of cardboard boxes dancing around by themselves would make more of an impression. At the very least, I thought she'd have a few questions—questions that would lead to my lab being discovered and the goo being confiscated and me being grounded for the rest of my natural life.

But, except for the noise, she was taking it all surprisingly well. So I just shrugged.

Mom rolled her eyes.

"Howard, shut off that music and come to bed," she told me, then she turned around and headed for the door. "And tell Reynolds to take off that ridiculous costume."

The door closed.

Reynolds? Whew! She thought the robot was Reynolds Pipkin—I was safe! I switched off the music, counted my blessings, and took the robot back into the lab. Before I left, I slid a sheet of plywood in front of the new robo-exit, sealing my secrets inside.

CHAPTER
15

The Trophy Machine

"Mr. Z, have you got a minute?" I said.

"Sure, Howard," he said. "I'll be right with you."

Mr. Z was manning the "welcome" table at the Robotics Fair. The welcome table was the first stop for science classes and tour groups who'd scheduled a sneak peek at the robots while they were still in the building stage. The actual Robotics Fair hadn't started yet but, when it did, it would be a three-day public event where crowds could roam the exhibit hall, attend lectures, and watch the competitors show off their robots. To be honest, the only days that mattered to me were the ones they set aside for judging and the awards presentation. I could hardly wait for those!

But I'd have to, for a while anyway. Since the exhibit hall was empty this time of year, the county let the Believer Achievers set up early and use the space as a workshop. So, for the past two weeks, robot-builders had been bringing in their entries, meeting the other contestants and swapping robo-secrets with their fellow BAs.

Mr. Z was writing something down on his clipboard. I cleared my throat, just in case he'd forgotten about me.

"Just another minute, Howard," he said.

Today, instead of a T-shirt, Mr. Z was wearing a red golf shirt with a collar. It had "BA" embroidered in cursive on the pocket.

"Nice shirt," I said.

"Thank you," he said, and kept writing. I guess he noticed I was still staring at him and tapping my foot, because he added, "I like your parka."

"Thanks," I said. But I didn't stop tapping.

Finally, he finished what he was doing and gave me his full attention.

"What can I do for you, Howard?"

"I'm here to enter the robot contest," I said.

Mr. Z's eyes narrowed, and he scratched the top of his head.

"Didn't you just withdraw from the contest?"

"Yes," I said. "Now I'd like to reenter."

"But you told me your robot ran away."

"He did," I said.

"Did he come back?"

"No. This is a different robot."

I smiled. Mr. Z looked very confused.

"You have another robot? What, like a backup robot?" he asked.

"Sort of," I said.

He laid his head back and stared at the ceiling.

"You understand, Howard, most people don't have extra robots just sitting around in their closet."

"This is my last one," I assured him.

"Howard ..."

Mr. Z let out a long, tired sigh and propped his elbows on the table. His tone was warm but firm, the kind of tone parents use when they have to explain to a small child why they can't have an elephant.

"I'm glad you're so excited about this competition. I really am. But I've tried to make it clear to you that this isn't a game. These aren't toys out there. These are actual, real, working robots. And the judges at these things can be ... well, some of them can be downright rude. They're robot snobs, and they don't like to have their time wasted. And I'm only telling you this, Howard, because I think you can be one of the best someday. And I'd hate to see you be embarrassed and get discouraged because you entered the contest before you were ready."

"Oh, I'm ready," I said. The grin simply would not leave my face.

He stared at me without saying a word. Then he shrugged and handed me the form. I took out a pen.

"So, Howard, where is this robot?"

"Right outside," I said. Then I sat down and started filling in the information. "Name of robot? M-O-N-S-T-E-R."

Mr. Z craned his neck until he could see out a wide window beside the front doors. He had a curious look on his face.

"Howard ... is your robot in a box?"

"No, that's him," I said.

His forehead wrinkled.

"Your robot is made out of boxes?"

"Just his body," I said. "The rest of him is made out of … other stuff."

He shook his head. "Howard, I don't think this is going to …"

"Robot! Come!" I yelled.

The outside door opened. In strolled a six-foot cardboard creature with blinking, twinkly lights and the words "Handle with Care" on his torso.

Mr. Z stood up. He looked stunned.

"It walks …" he said, as if he was trying to convince his own brain. "Howard, do you have any idea how difficult it is to make a machine mimic human walking?"

I shrugged.

"It wasn't all that hard," I said. "The hard part was making him do this."

I reached into my coat pocket and pulled out an iPod connected to a small, portable speaker. I hit Play.

"BOMP! BOMP! BOMP! BOMP!"

The robot began to move. His hose-like arms were above his head, and he swayed to the left and the right in perfect time to the beat.

"This is unbelievable!" Mr. Z shouted, moving in for a closer look at the dancing creation. "Howard, how did you do this?"

"Oh, you know, hard work, all that," I said, hitting the stop button on my iPod.

A crowd had started to gather around the welcome table. They were all staring at the spectacular, cardboard, voice-activated boogie-bot.

CHAPTER 16

An Alarming Discovery

I really thought having a robot would change my life. But except for hanging out at the Robotics Fair, life was pretty much the same. And by the same, I mean weird.

For instance, I don't know if you've ever had a snow-mato explode in your face, but it's a tough thing to get out of your nostrils. I found that out after Stick introduced it as the newest lesson in his pain-inducing bag of dirty tricks.

For those of you taking notes, a snow-mato is a squishy tomato packed inside a snowball. The sting is impressive. The splatter is unbelievable. When the attack was over, I looked like the test dummy in a red paintball factory. I must've blown my nose fifty times, but everything still smelled like pizza sauce.

Including me. So, naturally, when I saw Josh Gutierrez and Skyler Pritchard in the hall at school, I kept my distance. They were scary enough without my making them hungry.

I'd slipped past them and was on my way to my next class when the fire alarm sounded. This was a startling development, and not just because it was loud. It broke the rules.

Here's the deal: When it comes to fire drills, there's an unspoken agreement between kids and schools. We agree to march outside in an orderly fashion, and, in exchange, they let us out of class. Only this time, the bell rang in between classes. It wasn't fair! Unless, of course, there really was a fire, in which case the rules would go out the window, along with a number of my classmates. But I didn't smell any smoke, just the lingering scent of squishy tomato. So if this wasn't a real fire, what was going on? Everyone froze in place, looking surprised and confused.

Well, everyone except Trevor Duke.

Trevor just kept walking down the hall like he had somewhere to be. He didn't miss a step. Something about it seemed strange—and then it got stranger. While the

other kids were rushing out of the building, Trevor stopped at a window and looked outside. I started to leave, but then—he did something that made me padlock my eyes to him. He made

a peculiar gesture with his hands, like a signal. He was signaling someone outside the building! From the way he was acting, it seemed to me like he was trying to hide what he was doing, but it didn't matter. I saw what I saw. When Trevor turned around, he caught me staring at him, and, for a second, I thought he might pull the same move on me that he had pulled on Ernie Wilkins. But when I saw the look on his face, I realized it wasn't anger. It was fear.

Trevor ducked his head and raced out the door.

What was he up to?

I joined the rest of the kids outside, and we stood there freezing in our thin shirts and sweaters until Vice Principal Hertz blew his whistle.

"False alarm!" he yelled.

So there was no fire. That meant the only thing burning was my desire to solve the mystery of Trevor Duke.

CHAPTER 17

Formal Conversation

Trevor's behavior was definitely odd. But then again, so was Winnie McKinney's. Ever since the Winter Formal came up, she'd been impossible to talk to. At least to talk to like a regular person. So, when I saw her in the hall, I decided to change my approach.

"How's that Winter Formal coming along?"

Wendell had given me some advice about prombies: if you want to get on their good side, pretend you care about what they're doing.

"Oh, it's wonderful!" she chimed, as if I'd flipped on some secret happy-switch. "We've got a photographer, and she's got this big arch that looks like it's made out of ice. We're all going to have our pictures taken under it! And then G-Force says he can set up these lights that ... Oh, sorry. I forgot you don't care about stuff like that."

"No, no, I do!" I lied. "It sounds interesting. Especially

that stuff about Gerald. I really want to see what he comes up with because, you know, he's ... an electronics genius."

I almost had to spit to get the terrible taste out of my mouth. Meanwhile, Winnie studied me.

"So," she said cautiously, "what are you saying? That you want to come to the formal?"

"Oh ... I don't know. I hadn't really thought about it."

It was the wrong thing to say. In Prombie Land, no one thinks about anything *except* the formal.

"I'm not going to force you to come, you know," Winnie said, her voice getting chillier by the second.

"I didn't say you were."

"I was just checking, because you sounded like you wanted to come now. But if you don't—"

"That's not what I said!" I interrupted.

Winnie sighed. All the glitter and fanciness seemed to be wearing her down, and I had the strangest feeling she'd be glad when it was over.

"I'm sorry, Howard. I don't mean to get all ... psycho," she said. "Look, I know you think the Winter Formal is dumb, and maybe it is, and maybe I'm dumb for caring so much about it, but I do. It's just when I think of the decorations and the music and everybody all dressed up, it seems like it's going to make a real nice memory. And those are things you keep forever. I don't want to miss out on that, Howard. Does that make any sense?"

You know something? It sort of did. Which is probably the reason I said something really, really stupid.

"Winnie, can I come to the Winter Formal?"

Instantly, I wanted to cut out my tongue and stomp on it.

"Of course you can! I'll sign you up!" she said. Her eyes were the size of dessert plates. "It's going to be amazing, isn't it? I can hardly wait!"

"Me neither!" My fake smile was starting to get shaky.

"Great!" Winnie said. "Maybe I'll save you a dance."

"A dance?"

"Right. I mean, unless you don't want ..."

"No, I do. I do want," I said. My face felt so hot, I thought it might burst into flames.

"Awesome."

She smiled. It was that classic Winnie McKinney smile, the one that scrunched up her nose and took up the whole bottom half of her face. I'd really missed that smile.

Then she glided down the hall to go do whatever it is prombies do. As for me, I headed on home wondering if there was a painless way to break both my legs.

CHAPTER 18

The Terrible, Horrible Dance Lesson

"Katie Beth, how do they dance at proms?"

"Very, very badly," she said, not bothering to look up from her magazine.

I hope you don't get the wrong idea about my sister. She's not nearly as nice as she sounds.

Katie Beth was stretched out in the oversized, over-stuffed chair in our living room. A lot of people mistakenly think Katie Beth is harmless because she's made mostly of hair. By that I mean she is a little slip of a person surrounded by gobs and gobs of long brown hair. She wears big glasses because she thinks they make her look smarter, but they don't. They just make her look blind.

I approached her cautiously.

"What I mean," I said, "is what kind of dancing do they do?"

"No kind, they just dance," she muttered. "You know, they jump around, they move their feet, yadda, yadda, yadda. Why?"

"Well," I started, "they're having the Winter Formal and ..."

Katie Beth lowered the magazine. Her already magnified eyes were as big as spaceships.

"You're going to the Winter Formal?" she asked, her voice reaching that cruel zone between astonishment and outright laughter.

"I didn't want to!" I assured her. "But I was talking with this girl, Winnie McKinney, and—"

"You're going with a girl?" she screamed.

"No! We were just talking about stuff, like lighting and ice arches and things like that, and she said she might save me a dance."

This, apparently, was too much for my sister to contain. She leaped out of the chair.

"Mom! Howard's going to the Winter Formal with his girlfriend!"

My mom streaked into the room. Her mouth could easily have been mistaken for a train tunnel.

"My baby has a girlfriend?" she said.

"I do not!"

I wanted to go bury my head in the snow and not pull it out until spring.

"She's saving him a dance," Katie Beth told her.

The two of them grabbed hands and jumped up and down as if our carpet was some kind of flat, fun-less trampoline.

"What?" I asked, panicking. "Why are you saying it like that? Is a saved dance different than a regular dance?"

"You bet it's different!" Katie Beth grinned.

"Different how?"

I'm sure my face was as white as Mr. Jolly's.

"Now, now, it doesn't have to be different," Mom said. "It's just that it *can* be different."

"It can? What do I have to do?"

"Here," Katie Beth said, moving uncomfortably close to me. "Put your arms around me."

"What? I'm not doing that!"

"You're not doing it with me or you're not doing it with Winnie McKinney?"

Her grin was pure evil.

"I'm not doing it with anybody!"

Mom laughed.

"Don't be silly, Howard. It's just slow dancing."

"And this is fast running!" I said.

In seconds, I was out the front door and headed for the safety of my lab. But on the way, I heard something.

"Pssssst . . ."

Our euonymus hedge was hissing at me.

"Howard," a nasally voice whispered. "I have news."

I walked to the bushes. Reynolds Pipkin was crouched behind them.

"Reynolds, what are you doing back there?"

"I thought we were doing an undercover thing. Isn't that why you told me to follow Trevor Duke?"

"I didn't tell you to follow Trevor."

"You asked about him," he said.

"So? It was just a question. If I asked about your mom, would you stalk your mom?"

"Why?" he said, his face becoming deadly serious. "What's Mother doing?"

"Never mind. What's your news about Trevor?"

"I'll have to show you," Reynolds said. "Come on."

CHAPTER
19

Skatesville

I've always said if you want to find something, you go to Reynolds Pipkin. He's a good snooper. Even so, I didn't expect to follow him to this part of town. We were in a lonely, run-down, deserted area. It was the kind of place most people would call creepy.

But around here, everyone just called it "Skatesville."

Skatesville was the name of the old roller skating rink that closed when I was in second grade. The big aluminum, dome-shaped building was still standing. Rising up out there in the middle of a whole lot of nothing, it looked like an abandoned barn waiting for the cows to come home. Well, roll home—the cows at Skatesville would have wheels on their hooves.

I looked around. There was nothing to see but boarded-up buildings, rocks, and railroad tracks. I remembered how we used to pack this place on Saturday mornings. We'd have skate races and backward skate and a limbo contest, and there was a concession stand where you could buy candy or popcorn or drinks. But you couldn't take them on the skating floor or Mr. Charlie would yell at you. Mr. Charlie owned the place, and he was kind of an old grouch. But Skatesville was awesome! Or maybe it just seemed awesome because I was a little kid back then.

It sure wasn't awesome now. It was just a great big empty cave nobody had been inside in years.

"Reynolds," I whispered, because this was a whispering kind of place, "what are we doing here?"

"Watching," he said.

"Watching what? There's nothing out here."

"Look inside."

Inside? I didn't like where this was headed. It was one thing for Reynolds to go snooping around creepy old places— he looked like he belonged there. But I was a different story. With my cotton-white hair and bright, shiny braces, I practically glowed in the dark. Whatever horrors lurked in the shadows would see me coming from a mile away.

"Inside," Reynolds said again, blinking.

I guess my curiosity must have been greater than my fear because I noticed my feet were slowly moving toward the front doors. Reynolds was right behind me. As we crept closer, I saw something—a kind of a dull glimmer. There was a light on inside the building! The light was faint because Skatesville's glass front doors were tinted black, but where the tint had worn away, I could see an eerie glow. I bent over and peeked through the cracks.

Someone was in there. My view wasn't great and they were at the far end of the rink, but it was definitely a person. I squinted and strained my eyeballs until I could make out more. He was standing behind a sort of a weird-looking table. No, not a table—there were wires coming out of it. At that point, the figure raised his head, and I got my first clear view of his face.

It was Trevor Duke.

"He comes here every night," Reynolds said.

"What's he doing in there?" I asked.

"I don't know. But it's suspicious activity."

"How do you know it's suspicious activity?"

"Because I'm suspicious."

He had a point.

We turned and quietly slunk away. I was cold and frustrated. Instead of solving the Trevor mystery, this trip had only added to it. The whole situation was weird.

Fortunately, when it came to weirdness, I knew an expert.

CHAPTER 20

The Expert

"So this electronic table—would you call it a control panel?" Uncle Ben asked me.

"Maybe," I shrugged. "I couldn't see much."

"Hmmmmm."

Uncle Ben scratched his chin the way TV detectives do when they've just uncovered a clue. He was wearing his usual business clothes, which meant an untucked plaid shirt, torn jeans, and white high-top sneakers. His black hair hadn't been combed maybe ever, and his beard was just scruffy enough to look cool.

"I see," he said, looking back and forth between me and Reynolds.

I knew he'd still be in his shop. Uncle Ben's a night owl. Most days, he's up there until midnight or later because, well, when a place is this awesome, why would you go anywhere else? He owns Ben's Electro-A-Go-Go, a used-electronics store that sits in a mini-mall between a Vietnamese donut shop and a place that sells old records.

"Did you notice anything else?" he said.

"No," I said. "Except that he was wearing headphones. Is that important?"

"Well, when you say headphones," Uncle Ben said, "are you talking about those little earbud things, like on an iPod? Or are you talking about the big boys?"

He went to a shelf and grabbed a dusty pair of over-sized headphones. They looked like two green turtle shells connected by a curved stick.

"Kind of like those, I guess," I said. "Is that important?"

He scratched his chin again.

"Maybe. Maybe not. This set here is military-grade. They'd be used by someone doing battlefield communications or surveillance."

"Surveillance!" I said. "You mean like spying?"

Uncle Ben waved his hands in the air.

"Whoa, whoa! Nobody said anything about spies. All we really know is that somebody is listening to something in an abandoned building at night. And this happens to be the same individual who may or may not have set off a fire alarm to create a diversion so that he could signal an unidentified accomplice outside your school."

"And he knows karate. Or kung fu. Or something. Anyway, he flipped Ernie Wilkins in the cafeteria," I told him. "Does that mean anything?"

Uncle Ben raised an eyebrow.

"No," he said. "It's just . . ."

"Suspicious," Reynolds said.

They both stood there scratching their chins and nodding at each other.

If there's one thing my uncle loves, it's a good conspiracy theory. But if there's another thing he loves, it's a good joke. Which is why I wondered if he was messing with us. You never knew with Uncle Ben. He might seriously believe that Trevor could be a spy. Then again, he might just believe it would be seriously funny if we did.

"Come on!" I said. "He's just a kid. Do you really think a twelve-year-old could be a spy for another country?"

"Another country? No, no," Uncle Ben said, straightening the stuff on his counter. "Another planet."

All right, now I knew he was joking. Wasn't he? Uncle Ben goes to a lot of these sci-fi conventions, and he's seen just about every alien invasion movie there is, so he's kind of an expert on this stuff. But he didn't really think Trevor was an alien. Did he?

Reynolds reached for his inhaler.

"Relax," Uncle Ben said, breaking into a wide grin. "This guy's not an alien. You've seen the movies, Howard. If he were an alien, he'd be green and squishy, right? Does he look green and squishy?"

I shook my head.

"Well, there you go. Proof positive, he's not an alien spy reporting back to his intergalactic overlords. We can all rest easy tonight."

As much as I hated to admit it, I felt relieved. Reynolds was still sweating, but at least he was smiling now. Good.

This was going to make the trip home in the dark a lot less creepy.

"Unless he's an android," Uncle Ben said.

Reynolds gasped.

CHAPTER
21

Robot Invaders
from Mars

I could barely hold my eyes open at school the next day.
I'd sat up half the night with Reynolds—Uncle Ben's
comment about androids had him so worked up he
couldn't sleep. See, Reynolds is fine with ordinary robots,
but androids are robots that are made to look like people.
The suggestion that they might be real bothered him—
just not for the reason I figured.

"If a robot can look like a human, how do you know
you're not one?" he said.

I told him it was a ridiculous question … but between
you and me, I'm not ruling anything out.

So I more or less sleepwalked to school and yawned my
way through my classes. But as soon as the final bell rang,
I suddenly found myself wide awake and full of energy.
That's because I had something worth waking up for—
tonight, I was going to see *Robot Invaders from Mars*!

It was showing at the Mega-Monster Film Festival. And going to a movie at the Mega-Monster Film Festival isn't like going to a regular movie. At a regular movie, you just get to watch the movie. But at the Mega-Monster, you get to watch the weirdos!

Now, I'm not saying everyone who goes to the film festival is a weirdo. I'm just saying the weirdos are the only ones who are fun to watch. They all dress up like characters in the movies—monsters and aliens and mutants and machines. But they don't just dress like them. They like to pretend that they actually are those things! It's hilarious!

The weirdos are neat. Before them, I had always assumed that there would come a time in my life when, like all adults, I'd become boring. But the weirdos showed me that you can be a grown-up and still be interesting. You just have to imagine that you're someone else! Preferably someone with fangs or metal claws. In a lot of ways, it's like they are still kids. I mean, remember when you were little and you'd play superheroes, and you'd run around in your underwear with a towel for a cape? Last year, I saw six guys at the festival dressed just like that!

I bought my ticket and went inside the theater. The movie was awesome! There were these evil-looking space robots that were attacking the Earth. They'd chase people and breathe fire and shoot lasers out of their eyeballs. Of course, now that I'd actually seen robots up close, I knew they didn't really do stuff like that. They mostly just danced and played golf.

When I came outside again, the sun was nearly down.

The theater wasn't far from my house, but I still wanted to get home before it was completely dark. If scary movies have taught me anything, it's that nothing bad ever happens in the daytime.

I entered the alley next to the Bijou Theater, my usual shortcut, because it's definitely the quickest route home. But today, I don't know, it just seemed different. The alley was darker than it had been on the street. Quieter too. I found myself jumping at every little noise as I weaved through the maze of interconnecting alleyways behind and between shops.

But the worst part wasn't the darkness or the noise—it was the unshakable feeling that I was being followed. I picked up my pace and heard the sound of footsteps matching my speed. So I whirled around, and that's when I saw it—a long, black shadow moving toward me! I stood paralyzed as the shadow grew bigger and bigger. I could make out the thick arms and wide shoulders … and square head.

Square head?

It definitely looked like Monster! But what would my robot be doing downtown? I told myself it was impossible, that robots didn't just run off on their own. Which probably would have been easier to believe if my last robot hadn't done THAT EXACT THING just a couple days before! So instead of getting out of there, like any sensible person, I moved toward the shadow. Instantly, it turned around. I chased it, but all I could see in the dark was a boxlike blur. When the robot reached the end of the alley,

I got a good look at it under the street-light. Now I was more certain than ever—it was Monster, all right. He walked out onto the street, and for a moment I lost him in the crowd of movie-goers, forcing me to dash down the block searching for clues.

Finally, I caught a glimpse of brown, cubular cardboard on the other side of a tall hedge. I hesitated for a second, but when it turned, I could see these words: "Handle with Care." I knew it! Leaping through the bushes, I landed on the automated escapee, and we both fell to the ground.

Monster pushed me away with his big C-shaped, metal claws. Which was weird because Monster didn't have C-shaped, metal claws. Now that I thought about it, he didn't have aluminum-foil antennas, either. I bent over and took a closer look at the cardboard figure on the ground.

Uh-oh.

"Boward?" the box-man said.

Did you know they put "Handle with Care" on lots of boxes? Because it was news to me.

"Josh?" I said.

It was Josh Gutierrez from school. This was the same Josh Gutierrez who'd once beaten me up because it was a

Tuesday. No other reason, I was just his Tuesday beating. I stood there feeling sick and wondering what he was going to do to me now.

"Why did you tackle me?" he yelled, struggling to get his boxy costume vertical again.

"I'm sorry! I thought you were a robot."

"Well, duh!" Josh said, thumping his cardboard chest. "I'm going to see *Robot Invaders from Mars*. At least I *was* until you knocked me out of line! I'd been waiting for twenty minutes! Bad move, Boward!"

There are few things more humiliating than being beaten up by a large paper box. Josh put me in a headlock and proceeded to give me my first taste of robo-noogies. It was awful. But even more awful was the question that was rolling around inside my head: If Josh had been waiting in line for twenty minutes, who had I been chasing through the alley?

I finally slipped out of Josh's robotic death grip, but I couldn't shake the feeling that something was up. I turned around and ran all way to the Robotics Fair. A group of BAs were hanging around the entrance, but I rushed past them and made a beeline for Monster.

There he was, standing right where I'd left him.

I moved in closer and searched for signs of a chase. Did robots sweat? Did they get out of breath? Did their feet get dirty? It didn't matter. There was nothing.

I'd been so sure—the robot downtown looked just like him. It moved just like him! Then I noticed Richard Patel at the next work table.

"Have you been here long?" I asked him.

"A couple of hours," he said.

"Has my robot been here the whole time?"

Richard looked at me like I was nuts, and I probably was. Robo-noogies can't be good for your brain.

"He hasn't moved an inch, Howard. Is everything all right?"

I said yes. But I had a Monster-sized feeling I could be wrong.

CHAPTER 22

The PizzaDog Encounter

Of the many, many annoying things about Gerald Forster, the most annoying was that he thought he was an UP.

UPs are the most popular kids at Dolley Madison. They're a very exclusive group.

And, OK, I'll admit that Gerald got a lot more popular after his robot show at the science assembly. And maybe the UPs did let him hang out with them sometimes. But that's only because he did their homework! Look, Gerald was one of the smart kids—and smart kids were brains and nerds. And brains and nerds aren't friends with UPs! At best, they're like some kind of a pet. I didn't make the rules, but I sure had to live by them. And so did Gerald Forster.

But he wasn't. He was acting like he actually belonged with the popular kids. I mean, come on—did he really think the UPs liked him? UPs only liked themselves!

It was pathetic.

So naturally, when I saw him in the UPs' booth at the PizzaDog—my favorite pizza/hot dog restaurant—I felt it was my nerdly duty to set him straight.

"Hello, Gerald," I said.

"What do you want, Boward?"

His beady eyes glared at me.

"Nothing. I'm just surprised to see you here, that's all. I thought you'd be at the Exhibit Hall … with … the science kids. Everybody's down there working on their robots, trying to make them better. Because the contest is in three days, and, if you haven't heard, the competition this year is a whole lot hotter!"

I licked my finger and held it in the air like the number one. Then I made a sizzling "Sssssssss" sound.

The UPs looked stunned. Their mouths were open like tiny caves.

"What is a dweeb doing at our table?" Crystal Arrington asked.

Before I knew what was happening, Kyle Stanford and Josh Gutierrez were on each side of me.

"Hey K-man! What's up, J-dawg?" I greeted them in their own language. "Just thought I'd come over and hang with my buds."

It turns out that you don't get to call the UPs your "buds" unless they actually like you. I caught a quick glimpse of Gerald shaking his head, almost as if he was trying to warn me, but it was too late. I could already feel the hands on me.

I'd just broken one of the most important rules in "Howard's Secret Book of Middle School Survival."

Never, ever, ever draw attention to yourself!

They dragged me outside, and a second later I felt a temporary loss of gravity. Then something icy-cold touched my back—and that's when I knew!

They were punishing me with the cruelest of all the curses of winter—*the Abominable Snow Wedgie!*

While Dino Lincoln and Bulldog Busby held me in the air, Kyle and Josh began shoveling armfuls of snow into my underwear. Then, when my pants had blown up like a microwave popcorn bag, they grabbed my waistband and pulled.

I won't try to describe the sensation, except to say this must be how a regular wedgie feels to a snowman.

Anyway, it was cold and painful and humiliating and, thankfully, over. Quickly, the mob disappeared back into the restaurant. I lingered on the snowbank, waiting for my chance to defrost with dignity.

When the coast was clear, I waddled to the restroom.

I opened the door and looked around. As a middle school student, I know that a public restroom is just a swirlee waiting to happen. But this was an emergency. I stepped into a vacant stall, shut the door, and shook out an unbelievable amount of snow. For the record, underpants have an incredible storage capacity.

After a few minutes of drying time, I was frost-free and ready to rejoin the sitting world. But that's when the restroom door opened and I heard footsteps. Now, when you've been chased by as many people as I have, you get pretty good at recognizing your enemies by the sound of their steps. This wasn't the heavy-footed, bull-like trudge of a jock or the cool, graceful glide of an UP—it was more of a sliding, sloshing sound. And the sliding slosh was the walk of a slacker.

I peeked through the crack in the stall door. It was Trevor Duke!

Oh no! What was he doing here? Silently, I watched as he walked straight to the sink and looked into the mirror. But he didn't check his teeth or wash his hands like a normal person. Instead, he did the last thing I'd expect. He reached underneath his long, stringy black hair and pulled part of his head off!

It wasn't an ordinary piece of head; it looked like some kind of electrical device. He placed it on the edge of the sink, and I tried to get a better look at it. All I could see was that it was small and flat and had a short cord attached to it. Then he splashed some water on his face, reached under his hair, and pushed the device back into place.

When he was gone, I practically fell out of the stall. My knees were shaking, and I staggered out of the building. It couldn't be true. It just couldn't be!

Uncle Ben was right—Trevor was an android!

CHAPTER 23

Robot Crime Scene

I told Franklin and Reynolds that Trevor was an android, and they believed me because, well, Franklin and Reynolds believe everything. But something was bugging me. I mean, the whole point of aliens building an android would be so that it would look like a normal human being, right?

I wasn't sure Trevor looked human enough to be an android.

Anyway, I couldn't waste time worrying about an alien invasion. I had more important things on my plate. The final judging for the robot competition was in two days!

When I arrived at the exhibit hall, I saw Mr. Z standing on the other side of the room. He was talking to a policeman.

"Oh, Howard," he called. "Come here, will you? Officer Gentry wants to ask you a couple of questions."

Questions? For me?

"Were you up here late last night?" Officer Gentry asked.

Officer Gentry was about my dad's age, or maybe it just seemed that way because they both wore uniforms. He was shorter than Dad, and a little wider, and instead of my dad's black and gray hair, he had a blue hat.

"No, sir," I said.

"How about early this morning?"

I shook my head.

"What time did you leave yesterday?"

"Five ... no, wait, five thirty!"

I remembered I'd gone straight from the exhibit hall to the PizzaDog.

"Did you see anything suspicious? Anybody who looked like they didn't belong here?"

I shook my head. Everyone I saw looked pretty nerdy, which meant this was where they belonged.

He flipped his black notebook shut.

"There was some vandalism here last night, Howard," Mr. Z said.

"Is Monster OK?" I asked.

"Monster?" Officer Gentry said.

"My robot."

"Oh," he said. "I didn't know they had names."

"He's fine, Howard," Mr. Z said. "But I'm afraid Richard wasn't so lucky."

"There's a robot named Richard?" Officer Gentry said.

"No, that's the boy who built the robot," Mr. Z explained.

I felt bad for Officer Gentry. High technology can be confusing.

"Did anybody see anything?" I asked.

"No. Nobody was here when it happened," Mr. Z said. "So the police are just trying to figure it out."

"I don't think there's anything to worry about. More than likely, the culprit is going to turn out to be someone in town for that monster film festival," Officer Gentry said. "You know how it is—monsters, robots. They attract the same kind of people. No offense."

He said "no offense" because by the same kind of people, he meant weirdos.

"Can I go check on my robot now?" I said.

☆ ☆ ☆

Yellow police tape surrounded the area where Monster was standing, but they let me go in anyway. Twisted bits of metal were all over the floor.

Richard Patel was on his knees sorting through small, broken pieces. I saw a robot lying on its side. It was leaking hydraulic fluid.

POLICE DO NOT CROSS

123

"Is that Putt-Putt?" I asked.

Richard nodded.

"I'm sorry. How long did it take you to build it?" I asked.

"Five months."

"Can you fix it?"

He shrugged. "Maybe. But not in time."

"What are you talking about?" Gerald said. "We've still got two days. We'll make it. You're going to be in that contest."

He was on the floor sorting through the robotic remains. Four other BAs were down there too.

"We'll have Putt-Putt running again if we have to stay here all night," Jennifer Cruz said.

I was confused. These kids were stopping their own work to help Richard. Richard was a nice guy, but he was the competition. Then I looked at them and, for the first time, I sort of understood what Mr. Z meant when he said the Believer Achievers were about more than winning trophies. Don't get me wrong, I wanted to win. I wanted to win so bad I could taste it. But not if Richard wasn't able to enter.

I dropped down to the floor and began helping them pick up the pieces.

I'd been working for about an hour trying to reattach the small wheels that turned Putt-Putt's treads. Of course, before I could attach them, I had to find them. The robot's parts were scattered everywhere, so we'd all fanned out and scanned the floor like little kids on an Easter egg hunt. I'd found four of the wheels, Jennifer Cruz had found two, and two were still missing. But it was coming together.

I glanced at my watch. It was getting late. The huge building that had been filled with people a few hours ago was practically empty. Now it was just us and the robots. I was squatting on the floor trying to make tiny screws fit into tiny holes when I realized someone was looking over my shoulder. It was Mr. Z.

"Oh, don't let me interrupt you, Howard," he said. "You're doing a nice job."

He spoke quietly. I'd noticed that everyone had been speaking in those quiet, hushed tones, the ones you always hear in hospitals. Because, really, that's what the place felt like—a hospital for robots. We were visiting a sick friend, and nothing would be right until he was back on his treads again.

I knew Mr. Z didn't have to be here. He could have gone home when everyone else did. But of course he wouldn't. If we were staying, he was staying, and it wasn't just because he was an advisor or a volunteer or a teacher. It was because he was a BA.

Mr. Z was one of us.

"I'm really proud of you guys," he said. "It means a lot that you stayed for Richard. I know you've all probably got better ways you could be spending your evening."

I looked at him and raised an eyebrow. Was he kidding? Had he seen this crew? We were geeks! Techie, nerdy, pure, proud, united geeks! None of us had anything better to do that evening. Or any evening! How could we? What could possibly be better than spending the night working on robots?

"Hey, Boward," Gerald called to me.

It's funny, I'd almost forgotten Gerald was around. Normally his presence hovers over me like a dark, annoying cloud, but, for some reason, it was different here. Now that we were on the same team, he seemed … semi-tolerable.

"Yeah?" I said.

"Did you add anything to Monster today?" he asked.

"Today? No."

The truth was I hadn't added anything to Monster since I entered him in the contest. The other guys were constantly tinkering with their robots, trying to make them just a little bit better. But Monster was made mostly of goo—how do you upgrade goo? So whenever anyone was around, I pretended I was making adjustments or running a system check or something. It was a way to pass the time until I picked up my trophy.

"Mr. Z, I think you need to see this," Gerald said.

He was looking at Monster.

Mr. Z walked to where Gerald was standing, and I followed. Gerald pointed to something on Monster's back.

I looked and gasped. It was like I'd just been kicked hard in the stomach.

"Richard," Mr. Z said. "Can you come here for a second?"

Richard put down his soldering iron and joined us.

"Are these your solar cells?" Mr. Z asked him, pointing to the patch of glossy squares attached to Monster's upper back.

Richard stared at them, and then his eyes darted to me.

"Richard, I don't know how this happened!" I said. "I didn't do it!"

My outburst brought the entire group. They gathered together behind Monster, waiting for an explanation.

I didn't have one.

"I wouldn't break Putt-Putt. I'd never do something like that!" I said.

"Then how did those cells get on your robot?" Jennifer Cruz asked.

"I don't know!" I yelled.

It was a bad answer even though it was the truth. But what else could I tell them? That someone was setting me up? That they'd planted evidence on my robot to make me look bad? I couldn't say that—I didn't know that! All I knew was that I had questions that didn't have answers.

And the first one was, why was Gerald looking at Monster when we were supposed to be helping Richard?

I glared at him.

"We'll sort this all out later," Mr. Z said. "Let's get back to work now. We've got a lot to do."

I started walking back to my pile of wheels and hardware, but Mr. Z stopped me.

"Howard, I think maybe it would be best if you went on home now," he said.

"But I didn't ..."

"Go home, Howard," he said.

I looked around at the other BAs. Their eyes were already pushing me out the door.

I walked out feeling guilty for something I didn't even do.

CHAPTER 24

Mr. Z

All the clocks at school had stopped working. They must have—it just wasn't possible for time to move that slowly. It was prolonging the agony of being branded a robot smasher and a thief. I needed the bell to ring. I needed to set things right with Mr. Z.

Honestly, I was hoping it had been a bad dream. But then I saw Mr. Z's face in science class and, well, I quit hoping. He looked like he hadn't slept at all. Usually, Mr. Z likes to joke around and make his lessons fun, but this one was as dry as old paint. Worse, he never once called on me for an answer. I raised my hand and bounced up and down, but it was no use. I was invisible, a smudge on an empty desk.

When class ended, I kept my seat.

"Mr. Z …"

"After school, Howard."

That's all he said. So now I was trapped in an even longer prison of minutes waiting for my release.

Finally, the bell rang for the last time that day. I cleared the door at a run and was halfway down the hall to Mr. Z's room when I hit a roadblock. It wore a blue and white skirt with matching scrunchie.

"I need your help," Crystal Arrington told me.

"Maybe later. I'm in kind of a hurry."

Crystal's eyebrows came together in an angry V, but then they separated and her face broke into the sweetest smile good dental coverage can buy.

"Aw, come on. It'll only take a second. Pleeeeeeease!"

Crystal is conceited, pushy, manipulative, snobby, and rude. She's also a cheerleader.

"OK," I said.

I followed her to the gym. A group of girls was spread out on the floor surrounded by markers, glue, and every color of glitter in the sparkly rainbow. We stopped next to a long paper banner lying on the floor. It said:

DMMS WINTER FORMAL
7 PM FRIDAY
DON'T MISS THE MAGIC!

"I need you to put this up there," she said, pointing to a spot just below the ceiling.

"That's high," I informed her.

"Duh. Mr. McGinty is bringing a ladder."

Painful minutes passed before Mr. McGinty, the school janitor, arrived with a tall stepladder. Mr. McGinty is a nice man with a mustache that looks like it's made out of milk. He helps out with decorations and stuff sometimes, but I thought he was probably too busy and too old to be climbing the giant ladder. Besides, it wasn't his job.

His job was to clean up the mess when I fell off of it.

Crystal widened her dark brown eyes and looked at me.

"Up," she said.

"Ummmm, I have a little problem with heights," I confessed. "I get nosebleeds."

"Gross," she said. I'm pretty sure this is as close as Crystal ever comes to sympathy.

She tapped her foot. Reluctantly, I started the long, slow trek up the ladder. I could only use one hand to climb because I had to grip the banner in my other hand. The banner was so long, it fluttered around my toes like a huge glittery flag. I had reached the top and was dangling perilously from one side when I heard a voice below say, "It's a nerd, it's a plane—it's a flying brain!"

"Dino!" Crystal squealed.

Dino Lincoln had entered the gym. Dino is the captain of the basketball team and probably the most popular boy at Dolley Madison. He has this way of making everyday, ordinary things look cool. Like walking. Or sitting. Or wearing sunglasses.

Dino wears them indoors.

"What's How-Bow doing up there?" Dino asked.

"Ruining my banner," Crystal said. She glared up at me. "I told you not to wrinkle it!"

"Come on down from there, dawg," Dino said. "The A-team's here."

I gladly surrendered my place in the stratosphere and rushed down the ladder.

"Thanks!" I told Dino, and hurriedly turned for the door.

"Wait a second. We're not done here," Dino said.

Instinctively, my feet slammed on the brakes. I should have known I wasn't getting out that easily. I mean, Dino's not a bad guy—not compared to Josh and Kyle anyway—but he's still an UP. And UPs have a reputation to protect.

He summoned me with his index finger.

I didn't have time for this. Quickly, I reached back, grabbed hold of my own underpants, and administered a self-wedgie. Dino looked surprised—but only for a second.

"Nice form," he said. "But I would have made it atomic."

"Next time!" I yelled, and dashed out of the gym.

I ran down the hall until I was standing in front of Mr. Z's classroom. The door was closed. When it opened, Gerald Forster walked out.

I looked at him. He looked at me. We said nothing. Gerald turned his eyes down the hall and then followed them.

I went inside.

"Sit down, Howard," Mr. Z said.

I sat down in my regular desk. Mr. Z took the one next to it.

"How's Putt-Putt?" I asked.

"I think he's going to make it," Mr. Z said.

Then we both sat there in silence, wondering who was going to make the next move.

"Howard," he said at last, "what happened yesterday was very serious. It goes against everything Believer Achievers stands for. See, we try to live by a certain code—we treat other people the way we'd want them to treat us. In a way, we're kind of like a family. And families have to be able to trust each other."

"I didn't do it," I said, my voice cracking in a way I hadn't expected.

Mr. Z looked down at the desk, then back up again.

"I've spoken with the directors, Howard. They think it's best if you withdraw from the contest."

"Withdraw?"

"You don't have to leave the BAs," he said. "We don't want you to—we're not about turning kids away. And you don't have to worry. Nobody is going to say anything to the police—"

"Police!"

"Calm down, Howard. We just think, after what happened, a withdrawal would be best for everybody."

"I don't understand," I said. "You say it's best for everybody, but, to me, it sounds like I'm being punished. But how can you punish me for something I've told you I didn't do?"

Mr. Z closed his eyes.

"You don't believe me," I said. "No one believes me."

"It's not that, Howard. We don't want to punish you. It's just that they think—we think—there are certain lessons you need to learn before you're ready to compete with the others."

Compete? I was competing just fine until Gerald spotted those solar cells.

"But I already built the robot!" I said.

"I'm not talking about those kinds of lessons, Howard!" Mr. Z said, growing frustrated. "Look, from the very start, your only concern has been winning. Did you know I can tell you what went into almost every robot in that contest? That's because the kids can't wait to share it, to talk about it, to teach the others how to do what they did. But I don't know the first thing about Monster, Howard. It's like he's this mysterious toy that nobody gets to play with but you."

Looking at it that way, I guess I must have seemed pretty selfish. But the truth was, I couldn't tell Mr. Z how Monster worked. I didn't know how. He just did.

"I'm sorry, Howard. You built a fantastic robot, and you should be proud. I mean, that's your creation! But the thing is, Howard, you're a creation too. An incredibly gifted creation. What I'm trying to say is—do you really think you were given those gifts just so you could put a trophy on your shelf?"

What could I say? He was right. I did just want the trophy. But when I saw how everybody came together to help Richard, I don't know, something changed.

"I'll do better," I promised.

"I'm sure you will, Howard. But because of what happened, some of the kids have said they wouldn't be comfortable with you being there."

"You mean Gerald," I said coldly.

Now we were getting to the truth.

"Gerald? Howard, did you see G-Force leaving here?"

I nodded.

"This has nothing to with Gerald Forster."

"Oh really?" I said. "He didn't come in here to tell you that he wouldn't be 'comfortable' being in a group with a lying, robot-smashing thief?"

"What are you talking about?"

"Gerald. He's out to get me. He's been out to get me since I joined."

Mr. Z gave me an odd look and then a sort of a grin. But not the happy kind of grin.

"Howard, G-Force came here to defend you. He doesn't think you did it."

"What do you mean?" I said.

"He said it doesn't add up. For one thing, the solar cells on Monster were in plain sight where anyone could have seen them. And they weren't hooked to a battery, so there was no way to store the power. He said you were too smart to make stupid mistakes like that. But mainly, he said you couldn't have done it because that would be cheating. And Howard Boward doesn't cheat."

I felt sick and lost and ashamed. How could I have been so wrong about Gerald? And how could he have been so wrong about me?

Howard Boward did cheat. I cheated the second I opened the barrel and took out the goo.

"I'll withdraw from the contest," I said.

I got up and headed out of the classroom. The school was nearly empty now. Just before I reached the heavy exit doors, I heard Mr. Z's voice echoing down the hall.

"I believe you, Howard."

Welcome Home, Robot

If you're wondering, Gerald didn't win the contest. Putt-Putt did. I wasn't there but Reynolds was, and he told me all about it. He said Richard Patel made the whole group come up and accept the prize with him. It sounded nice.

Uncle Ben's red Toyota pickup pulled into the driveway. He drove to the rear of the house and stopped in front of the garage. I peeked into the back of the truck and saw Monster lying there like a stack of lumber.

"Wait a minute, I'll help you unload him," Uncle Ben said.

I'd had him pick up Monster at the exhibit hall for me. I didn't want to go back and face the BAs.

"I can handle it," I said. "Monster, get up!"

The robot bent at the waist and sat straight up, then climbed to his feet.

"Now get down," I said.

He stepped off of the truck, landing perfectly on the two dog bowls at the bottom of his legs.

Uncle Ben stared at me.

"You know, you might have mentioned he could do that before I broke my back loading him in there."

I laughed.

"How heavy could he be?" I said. "He's made out of cardboard."

"Cardboard? Howard, I don't know what that stuff is, but it ain't cardboard."

What was he talking about? Of course it was cardboard. I gave him a sideways glance, then walked over to the robot and tapped my fist against his chest.

It made a rumbling-drum noise, like when you thump the front of a washing machine.

He was right! It still looked like cardboard, but somehow it had transformed into something a whole a lot harder.

"That's weird," I said.

Uncle Ben closed the tailgate on his truck and leaned against it.

"Do your mom and dad know about this guy?" he said, pointing to Monster.

I shook my head.

I meant to tell them, I really did, but I couldn't. Not while the memory of Mr. Jolly still lingered in the air.

"I don't like to dump a lot of bad news on them at one time," I said. "I haven't even told them what happened with the BAs yet."

Uncle Ben nodded, then looked down at his sneakers.

"They asked about you," he said. "When I went to pick up the robot, a couple of kids were hanging around there. They wanted to know if you were OK."

I wondered which kids he'd seen, then remembered the way they'd all looked at me that last night at the exhibit hall.

"I'm awesome. Like always."

"That's what I told 'em," Uncle Ben said.

Then he climbed back into his truck and drove away.

☆ ☆ ☆

When I crawled out of the tunnel and into the lab, the first thing I saw was the banner.

"WELCOME HOME, ROBOT!" it said.

The banner was hand-painted on an old white bedsheet that hung from the ceiling.

"What is this?"

"I told him not to do it, Howard," Franklin said grumpily.

Franklin's large frowning face was displayed in full screen on the tablet, which was propped up on my lab table. He looked irritated. Probably because on top of the tablet, like a little crown, was a paper party hat.

This had Reynolds Pipkin written all over it.

Reynolds was standing at attention in the center of the room. He lifted a tiny plastic horn and blew it like a trumpet.

"Welcome, robot!" he said.

If Monster was moved at all by this presentation, he hid it really well.

"Reynolds, why would you throw a robot a homecoming party?" I said.

"I don't know. What kind of party are you supposed to throw for a robot?"

He blinked.

"Never mind," I said.

I told Monster to go stand in the corner. He obeyed.

"Howard," Franklin said, "it's probably best to go ahead and get it over with. You know, before you get too attached to him."

I cocked an eyebrow.

"What are you talking about?" I said.

Franklin seemed surprised.

"You know—getting rid of him? You said you were going to get rid of him as soon as the contest was over."

Oh, right. I did say that. But in my defense, I only said it because I thought the experiment had zero chance of working. I mean, who gets rid of a perfectly good robot? The truth was, I didn't even know how to get to the goo. That cardboard box had hardened like a turtle shell.

It was the ultimate superpower!

"Well, we'll see," I said, scratching my head. "A thing like that could take awhile. It's not like he has an off switch or anything. I'll probably have to use ... algebra."

Whenever I need to avoid doing something, I say I'm using algebra. It makes it sound complicated.

But Franklin wasn't listening. He was just glaring at Monster.

"He looks evil," he said. "Don't you think he looks evil?"

"That's how robots are supposed to look!" I said.

"He's dangerous, Howard. I don't like him."

I didn't know what to say. Franklin had always been a worrier, but it was worse now that he didn't have a real body. He couldn't protect me like he used to. I knew that it bothered him. Sometimes it bothered him a lot.

"I could keep him at my house," Reynolds said.

Finally, something that made me laugh!

"Your house? You can't even have goldfish!"

Reynolds blinked at me.

"Mother says they stare at her," he said.

CHAPTER
26

Bird vs. Nerd

When I came downstairs the next morning, the first voice I heard was Precious.

"Howard's a dork. BWAAAAK!"

"Shut up, Precious," I said.

Precious is a cockatoo, my mom's white-feathered bird-brat whom she has overstuffed to the point of near explosion. The problem with Precious, besides an insatiable appetite for crackers, is that she can talk. You'd think that would be a cool thing, but it isn't. Not when Stick is constantly feeding her new insults.

"BWAAAK! Howard's a creep!"

"Good morning, Precious," Mom said as she walked into the kitchen in her pink housecoat and fuzzy slippers.

"Howard stinks!" Precious squawked.

"Yes, Mommy knows," my mom said.

"Hey! The bird stinks, not me," I said.

Precious and my mom looked at each other. They both shook their heads. Mom opened the pantry and pulled out the pancake mix.

"Howard, do you think you could help us clean out the garage next weekend?" she said.

The garage? The lab! My heart stopped.

"Why … would you want to clean out the garage?" I gulped.

Mom grabbed a gigantic measuring cup and filled it with water.

"I'm thinking we need to be able to put the cars inside. There were some incidents last night."

"What kind of incidents?" I said.

"Well, Mrs. Johnson called this morning and said someone had broken the security light in her front yard. And, right across the street, they took Frank Nelson's electric snowblower and smashed it to pieces. They just smashed it! It's nothing serious, but she was warning us not to leave anything outside."

They smashed a snowblower? What was the deal with people smashing stuff all of sudden? I wondered if it was the work of some technology-hating gang.

"Who do you think did it?" I asked.

Mom shrugged.

"Sounds like some kind of sick loser," I said.

"BWAAAK! Howard's a loser!"

Mom handed her a cracker. I was beginning to think Stick wasn't the only one encouraging Precious's anti-Howard comments.

"You know who it probably is?" I said, remembering what Officer Gentry had told me. "It's probably just some weirdos in town for the Mega-Monster Film Festival. No use cleaning a whole garage over a bunch of weirdos who are just going to leave town in a few days."

Dad and Stick walked in. Dad was wearing a pair of vampire teeth, and Stick had on a Wolfman mask. They'd fallen asleep in the den watching a monster marathon. Without a word, they grabbed a couple of sodas out of the refrigerator and left again. Mom's eyes followed them.

"Not all the weirdos are from out of town, Howard," she said.

"But Mom!"

"Don't be lazy, Howard. The garage needs to be cleaned anyway."

"Don't be lazy, Howard," Precious echoed.

I stuck my tongue out at her. The bird laughed mockingly.

"You'll see. It'll be fun," Mom said. "We'll get Nathaniel to help you."

Nathaniel? Whew, I was saved. There wasn't a slacker anywhere on the planet who was better at getting out of work than Stick. Once he got a look at that clutter, there'd be—

I didn't finish the thought. I couldn't. My mind had been taken over by the sight of a robot in the backyard strolling by the kitchen window!

"Gotta run! No time for breakfast!" I yelled and made a mad dash for the front door.

Once outside, I ran to the rear of the house and located Monster. I placed both hands squarely on his back and pushed as hard as I could. Why did robots have to be so heavy? It took every ounce of my strength, but, finally, I got him away from the window. Then I coaxed him back into the garage.

"Bad robot! Bad, bad robot!" I told him. "I am very unhappy with you!"

Then I whirled around and faced the robot on my other side. "And you too!"

Not being a morning person, it took a second for my brain to process this new information.

There were two robots in my lab!

CHAPTER 27

The Art of Nerd Sliding

I sealed the lab door with the robots inside. I still couldn't believe it. I had two robots now—plural! If my parents found out, I'd be grounded for twice as long! What was killing me was that I didn't know where the second robot had come from. It just sort of—appeared. And it looked so weird. It had a box body like Monster's, but its arms were made out of pipes and its head was an old, metal bucket. How had this happened?

In a fair world, I'd have gotten to sit down and sort out this mystery with no distractions. Unfortunately, middle school is not a fair world.

It is a world of nerd sliding.

From what I know about nerd sliding, which is more than I wish I did, it works like this: two horrible creatures (let's call them Bulldog Busby and Kyle Stanford) select a "nerd" (let's call him Howard) and pick him up by his arms and legs. Then they swing him back and forth vigorously until he builds up a head of steam and—WHOOSH!—they send him sliding across the icy ground. Later, the nerd is judged for distance and accuracy.

I'm told the winner gets to choose the next nerd.

As you can see, it's not a complicated sport. But at Dolley Madison, it's very popular.

Which is why I felt the hair stand up on the back of my neck that morning when I saw the gathering of bullies on the school lawn.

"Boward, come here!" Bulldog Busby screamed. "We need your help with something!"

Instantly, I knew I did not wish to provide the kind of help Bulldog needed. Nerd sliding is hard on the rump, and mine was still pretty chapped from the Abominable Snow Wedgie. So I realized my best course of action was to put as much distance between me and the sliders as I could. Sure, there was a good chance they'd catch me—but there was an equally good chance they'd come across another nerd before that happened.

And you know what they say: a nerd in the hand is worth two in the bush.

So I ran. To my surprise, I actually made it around the corner of the school without being caught, which was farther than I usually get. But winter was clearly on their side. When I hit the sidewalk, my feet slipped on the ice and I power-slid into an unknown object.

Except that it wasn't unknown. Or an object. It was

Trevor Duke. The impact sent him plunging face-first into a snow-bank by the cafeteria steps.

When Trevor got up, he started furiously shaking the snow from his ears. His eyes turned on me with a look of rage.

"I'm sorry!" I yelled. "I was just trying to get away and then I … I … I …"

But there was no time for explanations. My pursuers grabbed me from behind, and seconds later I was sliding like a hockey puck across a long and unpleasant stretch of ice. It felt like I was speeding butt-first through a field of frozen cactus.

When it was over, I climbed to my feet and shook off the snow. I could see Trevor watching me from the school doors … and I didn't think he liked what he saw.

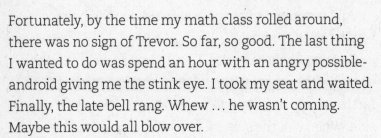

Fortunately, by the time my math class rolled around, there was no sign of Trevor. So far, so good. The last thing I wanted to do was spend an hour with an angry possible-android giving me the stink eye. I took my seat and waited. Finally, the late bell rang. Whew … he wasn't coming. Maybe this would all blow over.

But just when Mrs. Washington was about to start the lesson, the door opened. Trevor walked inside. It was like something out of a cowboy movie where the bad guy suddenly barges through the saloon doors. He handed Mrs. Washington a hall pass and then headed straight for me. But he didn't look at me. He just strolled by and dropped a folded piece of paper on my desk. I opened it.

"Meet me after school by the band room and I'll teach you a lesson," it said.

CHAPTER 28

To Flee or
Not to Flee

"You're not seriously thinking of meeting him?" Winnie
said.

I'd caught up with Winnie between classes and told her
about my Trevor trouble.

"I don't know."

My answer surprised even me. I mean, every instinct in
my soon-to-be-broken body was telling me not to go. And
yet, I thought I might.

"He'll obliterate you. Complete and total destruction,"
Winnie said.

"Probably," I said.

If there's one good thing about getting beat up as often
as I do, it's that it's incredibly educational. See, there are
all different kinds of bullies. After a while, you get sort of a
feel for how to handle them. For example, you avoid guys
like Josh and Kyle for as long as possible. That's because

they have short attention spans and lose interest as soon as the next shiny object crosses their path. If you can hide for two, three days tops, you're usually in the clear. But Trevor was not like Josh or Kyle or any bully I'd ever encountered.

Trevor could do math.

And, more importantly, he could do it correctly. That meant he had a good amount of patience. Avoiding him might only make his anger grow. Personally, I've always believed that it's better to take a mini-thrashing today than to wait and take the full-blown mega beat down later on.

Still, showing up was a risky move. Trevor was big. And he appeared to know some kind of kung fu or something. Plus, he had that android-thing in his head.

I've got to tell you, I'd feel really stupid if I showed up and the first thing he did was melt my face with his laser eyes.

"Howard, promise me you won't go," Winnie said. The look on her face was pleading.

"All right, Winnie. I promise."

What else could I say? Winnie had made a sincere request, and going to meet Trevor after that would have been a complete betrayal of our friendship. Also, there was a very good chance he'd kill me.

☆ ☆ ☆

When school was over, I rushed out of the building as fast as I could and started for home. I mean, I wasn't exactly looking forward to facing the robot brothers, but it was better than facing Trevor.

Speed was my best defense. If I could make it off the school grounds, I'd live for another day. Unfortunately, my escape route was being blocked by a mob of pint-sized cookie sellers.

"Are you Howard Boward?" a girl in pigtails asked me. She looked like she was about eight years old.

I stared at her suspiciously. She was small and blonde and wearing a brown and teal uniform. They were all wearing uniforms.

"Yes," I said.

"I'm supposed to give you this."

She handed me a note. I opened it.

"Never underestimate the size of your enemy," it said. "There is strength in numbers."

"Stick!" I muttered.

Then I looked back at the scouts. They were glaring at me.

"Let's get him!" the pigtailed one yelled.

The next thing I knew, all the girls were screaming and launching snowballs. I tried to run away, but they chased me. I didn't know how many cookies Stick had to buy to make this happen, but I was guessing it was a lot.

Finally, I lost them, and I ducked behind one of the school's portable buildings and waited for them to pass. I took a deep breath and held it until I knew I was safe again.

And that's when an arm wrapped around me and squeezed my neck like a vice.

CHAPTER 29

The Lesson

Instinctively, I threw myself backward into my attacker.

"No!" he commanded, grabbing my hand and placing it on his elbow. "Here."

Then I felt a pressure—but not the crushing kind—coaxing me to lower my hips.

"Now pull," the voice told me.

So I did.

A second later—against all laws of gravity and common sense—a body flipped over me and landed in the snow. It was attached to the face of Trevor Duke.

"I'm sorry!" I yelled, for some reason feeling the need to apologize for doing exactly as I was told.

Trevor nodded. Then he picked himself up off the ground and dusted the snow off his black leather jacket.

"Again?" he asked.

I was stunned. Trevor Duke was asking if I wanted to toss him again. And the thing was—I kind of did. It was fun, like playing ninja. There had to be a catch.

Cautiously, I nodded.

Trevor moved behind me. He adjusted my grip and said, "Now."

The result was the same, only this time I helped him up off the ground.

We tried it a couple of more times. It was getting easier. I didn't know what I'd been so worried about—I could toss this guy around all day! Then, after one particularly spectacular throw, I had to ask. "Why are you showing me this?"

Trevor shrugged. "I saw what those guys did."

I knew who he meant—Bulldog and Kyle. Trevor had seen the nerd sliding competition. Looking back, he hadn't been staring at me at all—he was staring at them. And he hadn't liked what he saw.

Funny, I'd never thought about how bullying could bother someone who wasn't on the receiving end of it. Maybe that's because I'm always on the receiving end of it.

"So, is this what you meant in your note when you said you were going to teach me a lesson?"

Trevor nodded. A wave of relief rushed over my body. It was a karate lesson! Trevor Duke was not going to melt my face with his laser eyes! I was going to live!

"Why didn't you just say so?" I said.

He shrugged.

"I don't like to talk in front of people."

"Why not?"

Trevor looked puzzled. It was the way Stick looks when there's only one donut left in the box and I ask him if he wants to split it. Of course he doesn't want to split it— he wants to eat it!

"My voice," Trevor said at last.

His voice? What was wrong with his voice? Sure, he had a little bit of an accent, but it wasn't bad. You could barely even tell he was an alien.

"What about it?" I said.

Trevor looked confused again, like there was something I wasn't getting.

"I'm ..."

But he didn't finish his sentence. Because at that moment, we both saw Winnie McKinney. She'd been standing across the courtyard watching us. Slowly, she walked up to us. Then she lifted her gloves and made a series of quick moves with her hands. It was a message, the kind I'd seen Trevor making at the window.

Trevor nodded and signaled back.

"I didn't know," she told him.

"Know what?" I asked.

"I'm deaf," Trevor said.

☆ ☆ ☆

The three of us left the school grounds and found ourselves walking together—me on one side, then Winnie, then Trevor.

"So, let me get this straight—you're not an alien android?" I blurted out.

Trevor shook his head. "No. But that would be pretty cool."

Winnie's eyes narrowed. She looked painfully confused.

"An android?" she asked me. "An android, Howard? Why would you even think that? What kind of a person just naturally assumes someone is a mechanoid from another planet?"

"I didn't just assume it," I said. "I had evidence. I saw him take part of his head off."

"You saw that?" Trevor said.

"Yeah. It was awesome!"

From the look on Winnie's face, I thought her brain was going to explode.

It turns out Trevor has something called a cochlear implant. It's an electronic device that allows some deaf people to hear sounds. The part I saw him remove in the PizzaDog bathroom was just the receiver.

"It's on the outside, but it attaches magnetically to the implant in my head," Trevor explained.

"There's more inside your head?" I yelled.

He nodded.

"Trevor Duke, you just got a thousand times cooler!"

Trevor laughed. Winnie just shook her head.

I asked about the hand signals, and Trevor showed us how to sign a couple of words. He called it American Sign Language. Winnie already knew a little because she has a deaf cousin.

"She's taught me a few things," she said. "Not very much. I can just say simple stuff like, 'My name is Winnie.'"

Trevor cocked his eyebrow.

"Actually, you said, 'My name is Winifred,'" he corrected her.

"Winifred!" I squealed.

"So?" Winnie said. "My cousin calls me Winifred. Big deal! That's where 'Winnie' comes from. What did you think? That I was named after a stuffed bear?"

"Maybe," I said. "I was named after a chimp."

"Howard is a chimp?" Trevor asked.

"No, I mean my middle name. Enos. He was the first chimpanzee to orbit the Earth."

"Enos!" Winnie was laughing so hard she nearly fell into a snowbank. "Wow! Your parents must really like the space program!"

"No," I said. "They just like monkeys."

CHAPTER
30

Children at Play

We passed the street where Winnie would have normally turned to go home. But she kept walking with us. I understood. The fact is, we'd passed my turn three blocks back.

It's just that now that Trevor was talking, and I was reasonably sure he was human, I wanted to know more about him. I guess Winnie felt the same way. If that meant we'd end up taking the long way home, that was a pretty small price to pay.

"Hey, Trevor, there's still one thing I don't understand," I said. "You remember that day the fire alarm went off and I saw you at the window? What was the deal with that?"

Trevor rolled his eyes. "I just didn't hear it," he said. "See, until I came here this year, I've always gone to the school for the deaf. So I'm not used to so much noise. Sometimes it's just too much, and I have to turn off my implant for a while. Anyway, I turned it off that day, and I didn't hear the alarm."

"But who was outside the window?" I asked.

Trevor looked like he wanted to crawl into a hole. "My mom," he groaned. "She's deaf, and she worries about me being at a hearing school. I told her it was fine, but you know … moms. Anyway, every day between second and third period, she stands out behind the cafeteria, and I have to come to the window and sign to her that I'm OK. It's so embarrassing!"

"Embarrassing! It's like a secret code! Why would you be embarrassed about that?"

"Because I'm in seventh grade! And my mom comes to school to check on me! Wouldn't you be embarrassed?"

I shook my head.

"You don't know my mom. She does way more embarrassing stuff than that," I said.

We laughed, and we walked, and finally, we ended up on Lamar Street about three blocks from the PizzaDog. Considering what happened the last time I was there, I felt a little nervous.

Then I saw him. A boy was at the end of the street waving his arms like a panicked swimmer. We ran to him. It was Gerald Forster. His tongue was frozen to the pole of a street sign.

The sign said, "CAUTION: Children at Play."

Gerald was bent over in an uncomfortable-looking position, and I wondered how long he'd been that way.

"Are you stuck?" I asked.

Winnie punched me in the shoulder. She's stronger than she looks.

"Of course he's stuck!" she said. "Do you think he'd be standing like that if he wasn't stuck?"

"Should we pull him loose?" I said.

"No," Trevor said. "Have him breathe on the pole. His breath is warm, and that should thaw him loose."

"Right," Winnie said. "G-Force, just breathe on it. Breathe heavy, like you're fogging up a mirror."

The three of us stood around him making breathing noises like panting dogs. But it was no use. He was too scared, and his breaths were short and panicky.

"I'll stay here. You two run to the PizzaDog and bring back some warm water," Winnie said.

Trevor and I started sprinting down the street.

"Make sure it's just warm, not boiling!" she yelled after us.

When we entered the PizzaDog, I did everything possible to make sure I avoided eye contact with the UPs. What's weird is that Trevor did exactly the opposite. While I ordered the warm water, he locked his eyes on their booth.

The UPs didn't stare back.

That's when I figured out what Trevor already knew— Gerald hadn't done this to himself.

We ran back to the signpost and handed Winnie the water. She slowly poured it over Gerald's tongue. It took a couple of minutes, but he was able to pull free.

161

"What happened?" I said.

"Nothing!" Gerald snapped. "The guys made me put my tongue on there, that's all. They were just playing around."

"Doesn't look like they were playing," Winnie said.

"Those guys are my friends!" Gerald told her.

Trevor looked down the street toward the PizzaDog.

"Then why aren't they here?" he asked.

Gerald was embarrassed and angry, and the only reason I know that is because I've felt that exact same way a hundred times before. I wouldn't have believed it was possible, but I actually felt sorry for Gerald Forster. And not just because of what happened with his tongue.

He'd thought he was one of them.

"I gotta go," Gerald said gruffly, then walked quickly to the corner. But he stopped before he got there and turned back to face us.

"Thanks, you guys. Thanks for helping me."

He disappeared around the corner, and the three of us started walking again.

"It's not fair," Winnie said. "Somebody needs to do something about those guys."

Which was funny. Because I'd just been thinking the same thing myself.

The Plural of Robot

I've always thought of my lab as a sanctuary, the place where I go to get away from my problems. But now that two robots were inside waiting for me, it felt different. I dreaded the trip through the tunnel. What could be worse than coming out the other side and staring into the cold, glassy eyes of two robotic faces?

I opened the dryer door … and found out.

There were five robotic faces.

Five robots were in my lab! They were multiplying! This was a disaster! It was just a matter of time before they filled up the lab and spilled out into the countryside. And I knew what came after that—robot world domination and the enslavement of the human race!

I couldn't let that happen. I'd be grounded for the rest of my life!

I heard a noise behind me and nearly jumped into the rafters. But it was just Reynolds coming out of the dryer. He looked around.

"Something's different," he said.

Pipkins are nothing if not observant.

"They're multiplying!" I screamed.

I was getting a crash course in robot math, and it wasn't a problem I could solve with a calculator. Two of the new robots were made of boxes and hoses, so they looked an awful lot like Monster. The third looked completely different. It had an old filing cabinet for a body and a paint can for a head.

"What do you think happened?" Reynolds asked.

"I don't know," I said. "But I'm stopping it now."

Franklin was right; I shouldn't have used the goo. It was time to put it in a barrel and seal it up forever. I grabbed one of the new robots and pulled at the cardboard flaps. The box wouldn't open. Quickly, I picked up a screwdriver and tried to pierce the thick, paper body. But I couldn't. It wasn't paper anymore. It was tough and leathery. So I whirled around and yanked on the drawer of the freaky-looking filing cabinet. It didn't budge.

No matter what I tried, I couldn't get to the goo. It's like it was protecting itself!

"You got any ideas?" I asked Reynolds.

"They could stay at my house," he said.

OK, I was getting pretty tired of Reynolds acting like robots were big, mechanical puppies.

"This is serious!" I said.

"Well, maybe you could sell them to people," he said. "They could be security guards. You know, because of the smashers."

"What smashers?" I said.

But I was only half listening. My mind was already calculating how many robots I could hide upstairs in my closet.

"The smashers. I saw it on the news. They've been breaking stuff all over the city."

Breaking stuff? Could that be who broke Mr. Nelson's snowblower? And Putt-Putt? I wanted to ask more about these smashers, but something more urgent came up. One of the robots had pulled off its head!

My mouth fell open. Reynolds was pumping his inhaler like a Pez dispenser.

Then I saw another robot grab a large cardboard box and dump the contents on the floor.

"Hey, that's our stuff!" I said.

It didn't care. It simply took the empty box and sat it down next to the headless robot. What happened after that still gives me nightmares. The headless robot bent over, and a stream of gooey, sticky ooze poured out of its neck. The goo landed in the empty box.

I felt queasy.

The rest of the robots began searching the garage. They brought back hoses and pipes and gloves and hooks, and they attached them to the goo-filled cube. When they'd finished, the lab had a brand-new robot.

Now, I'm not saying it was a perfect robot. It had a tea kettle for a head. But still, it was another robot!

I understood what was happening now. The robots were building new additions to the family using the goo from their own bodies. And they were building them out of junk in our garage! From a scientific standpoint, it was fascinating, but from every other standpoint, it was horrible!

"That's six," I muttered. "What am I going to do with six robots?"

"Maybe you could have them build you a bigger garage," Reynolds said.

It was a terrible idea. But he was right about one thing—this lab wasn't big enough for me and the robots.

"Reynolds, can I borrow your cell phone?" I said.

He handed it to me. I dialed Uncle Ben.

☆ ☆ ☆

Luckily, Stick had a hockey game that night. The whole family usually went to Stick's games, but nobody was surprised when I asked to stay home. After all, it involved Stick, ice, and sports—three things I try really hard to avoid. Still, it couldn't have come at a better time, because it gave me a couple of family-free hours to clear my lab of robots.

When everyone was gone, Uncle Ben pulled his truck to the back of the house. The great thing about Uncle Ben is that he acts normal even when things are totally weird. Like when I asked him to come over and pick up six robots, he just said, "Sure," like I'd asked him to drive me to Little League or something.

"Hey, squirt," he said. "What's the trouble?"

"Just look!" I said.

He glanced at the small army of mechanical monsters surrounding me.

"Oh yeah, the robots. Let's get them out of here."

We loaded them up and drove to the Electro-A-Go-Go.

"You're sure this is OK?" I said. I felt bad about asking my uncle to babysit these things.

"It's fine. I've got a lot of room in the back," he said.

I nodded. But the more I thought about it, the more my insides ached.

"Uncle Ben. Do you think we ought to … call somebody?"

"Who? Robot exterminators?"

"I don't know," I said. "Maybe the police? Or the FBI? Or the army?"

Uncle Ben looked at me, then rubbed his hand across his sandpaper-like beard. "Well, I guess we could call somebody," he said. "I mean, if that's what you want. Of course, the first thing they'll do is evacuate the neighborhood and put it under one of those big plastic tents they use for chemical spills."

"Really?" I said.

I'd never thought about that.

"Oh yeah. But not for long—just until they demolish your house. That's the center of the contamination zone. But that should be about it. I mean, they're not going to put you in jail or anything. They'll probably just send you to some secret government-genius facility, like the one where they keep the psychics and the super-intelligent monkeys."

I swallowed hard.

"I don't want to live with monkeys!" I said.

Uncle Ben smiled. "Then I guess this stays our little secret. Don't worry, Howard. We'll figure it out."

I looked around at the back of my uncle's shop. It was bigger than the lab, but it wasn't huge. If the robots kept multiplying, they'd outgrow it in just a few days.

"It's not going to work, is it?" I said.

"We'll see. Maybe there won't be any more of them," he said. "Of course, the real problem with this place is that it's a store. People are in and out all day. I wish I had a great big building, like a warehouse, somewhere nobody would go snooping around."

He was right. That was exactly what I needed. And it gave me an idea.

"Uncle Ben, can you give me a ride?"

CHAPTER 32

The Hokey Pokey Place

We pulled up in front of Skatesville. The huge electric sign on the roof looked as dark and cold as the rest of the place. I remembered how it used to light up the sky for miles.

Uncle Ben parked across the road.

"So you're going to go talk to that kid you told me about?"

"Yeah," I said.

"And you're sure he's not a spy or an alien or anything?" Uncle Ben sounded disappointed.

"Nope. Just deaf," I said.

He shrugged.

"Oh well. At least we've still got robots. You want me to wait for you?"

"No, I can make it home. Thanks, Uncle Ben."

I got out, and the truck made a wide U-turn on the dusty dirt road. I watched the taillights disappear over the hill, then walked to the door of the old roller rink.

It was unlocked. I stepped inside.

"Hello!" I yelled.

My voice ping-ponged around like I was in the belly of a great, aluminum whale.

I took a long look. The place had the same dim glow I'd seen when I was here with Reynolds. It made my shadow look huge. For a second, I imagined I was a roller-skating giant getting ready to take the floor and do the Hokey Pokey.

The Hokey Pokey. Man, I used to love that stupid dance!

I walked out to the middle of the rink and let my eyes soak up the memories. There in the corner was the concession stand, right where I'd left it. The candy on the shelf was long gone, but I could still see the white plastic sign that said "Popcorn—50 cents." I looked at the wooden floor. It needed a good cleaning. So did the red railing that made a big oval around the skate area. But I had a feeling that if you got rid of the dust and wiped off all the dirt, underneath you'd find the same old magic that used to make Mr. Charlie's place something special. I closed my eyes, and, just for a minute, I was in second grade again.

I put my right hand in.

I took my right hand out.

I put my right hand in.

And I shook it all about.

"Howard? What are you doing?"

It was Trevor's voice. His words caught me somewhere between my Hokey and my Pokey.

"Oh … hey, Trevor."

He was standing at the far end of the rink, decked out in a white T-shirt and gray cargo pants. Without the leather jacket, he looked smaller, more like a kid. He walked toward me.

"Just a second," he said.

Trevor put his hand under his long black hair and attached the magnet to the side of his head. He could hear me now.

"I was just … in the neighborhood," I said.

He looked confused. Nobody just happens to find themselves in Skatesville. So I explained how Reynolds had followed him here—because, you know, he's the biggest snoop in town—and how we'd stood outside and watched him doing something with the big electronic table in the corner. As I talked, the lines in his forehead got deeper and deeper and his lips pushed together until they were skinny and tight. By the time I'd finished, Trevor's face looked like a clinched fist.

"You were spying on me?" he asked.

For a minute, I thought he might punch me, or tell me to leave, or both. And I wouldn't have blamed him. Now that I'd gotten to know Trevor, my suspicions seemed pretty creepy.

"I'm really sorry," I said. "We just got caught up in … the mystery."

Trevor's eyes were still shooting death rays, but his jaw had started to loosen a little. After a few seconds, I thought I saw the first traces of a grin.

"Well, I guess we can call it even," he said. "I mean, I did just spy on you while you were doing the Hokey Pokey."

My face turned as red as the snow-mato stains on my parka. We both laughed out loud.

Trevor, it turns out, is Mr. Charlie's grandson. When Mr. Charlie died, Skatesville closed down, but now Trevor's mom was hoping to start it back up again.

"I don't know if it'll ever happen," he said. "The place needs a lot of work, and it's just the two of us. We do what we can on the weekends, but it's pretty slow going. Maybe someday."

I felt bad for him. I knew he wanted to help his mom, but Skatesville was a real mess. I mean, all I have to do is clean my room, and that still feels like the most gargantuan task ever faced by mortal man. Maybe that's why it never gets done.

"If you don't mind me asking," I said, "what were you doing with that thing?"

I pointed to the table in the corner with the wires running in every direction.

"Oh. That's just my board," he said. "It's for music. I do some sound mixing, some sampling, some deejay stuff. Things like that."

"Music?" I said.

"What? You think a deaf guy can't like music?"

"No, it's not that!" I said. "But … you do?"

He laughed.

"Yeah. Lots of deaf people do," he said. "I used to deejay some dances back at the deaf school."

"Dances?"

He shot me a weird look.

"Yeah, dances. Deaf people dance, Howard. We feel the beat, the vibration. Deaf dances are crazy fun!"

"I knew that," I said, but I didn't. "Did you know Beethoven was deaf?"

Trevor rolled his eyes.

"Yeah, Howard. I know about Beethoven," he said. "There are a lot of deaf musicians. You ever hear of Sean Forbes? Mandy Harvey? Signmark?"

I shook my head.

"You should check them out; they're good. And I don't mean deaf-good, I just mean good."

"Cool," I said. "What about you? Are you good?"

He shrugged.

"Mostly I just play around. I put different pieces of music together, maybe lay down some tracks of my own."

He put his fingers on a keyboard that looked like a piano and ran them to the end. The keys sounded like a bunch of different instruments.

"That's awesome," I said.

Trevor smiled and pushed a button. A song started. The speakers were really loud inside the big, empty building, which Trevor said was a good thing. Then he put his hand on a record and started spinning it back and forth to make a scratching noise. At first, it just sounded like something was broken. But once I got used to it, I really liked it.

"Hey, you're pretty good!" I said.

He shook his head.

"No, other guys are way better."

"You know what you should do?" I said. "You should play at the Winter Formal. They'd go nuts!"

Trevor just grinned at me.

"The Winter Formal is tomorrow, Howard."

It was? I'd been so busy with robots, I hadn't been watching the calendar.

"Well," I said, "you should still do it. You said you've done dances before."

"Yeah," he said. "But it's easier playing at deaf dances."

"Why?"

Trevor gave me a puzzled look. "Because they can't hear you," he said.

Oh yeah. I guess he had a point.

I left Skatesville and headed home without ever saying a word about the robots. I couldn't ask, not after I found out Trevor and his mom were trying to clean the place up so they could re-open the skating rink. They didn't need six robots messing up Skatesville even more. This was my problem, and I was the one who needed to deal with it.

CHAPTER
33

News Flash

Dad and Stick had left to go to another movie at the Mega-Monster Film Festival downtown, and Mom and Orson went to buy me a handkerchief to match the tie I was wearing to the dance. For some reason, it's considered bad manners to blow your nose in something that isn't color coordinated.

So now there was nobody in the house except me and Katie Beth. Weird how it still felt too crowded.

"So, the big formal is tonight," Katie Beth said.

She had an enormous grin on her face. It was creeping me out.

"I know," I said.

Then I returned to my pre-formal meal—a huge bowl of Choco-Socko cereal with extra sugar on top.

"Are you going to dance?"

Now she was hovering over me. The hovering was worse than the grinning.

"Why do you care?" I said.

"I don't. I just think it's sweet."

"Ewwwwwwww! It is not!" I said.

"Fine!" she said. "I was just trying to be nice, you little twerp."

That was better. At least she was calling me names. Now I could eat in peace.

Still, that was a good question. Was I going to dance? If I didn't dance, Winnie would probably be mad. But if I did, my social life was over. I wished I didn't have any choice, that I was like my boogie banana and would just start bouncing up and down the minute I heard music. But I wasn't. I was Howard Boward, master of the floppy arms and ninja kicks.

It was going to be a long night.

Katie Beth had left the TV on in the living room, and I could hear the news. They were talking about the smashers and all the vandalism that had occurred around town.

"Police think copycat vandals may be responsible for the random acts of property damage in the city," the news guy said. "But one local woman believes there's another explanation."

I leaned forward in my chair so that I could see the TV from the kitchen. There was a lady on the screen with orange hair and matching skin.

"It was a robot," she said. "At least that's what it looked like. I live right over there, and I saw it walking down the

176

street carrying a car battery. Well, then it stopped and put the battery on the ground and, a second later, sparks flew up everywhere. So I woke up my husband and I said 'Duane, there's a robot outside smashing car batteries!' Of course, he just rolled over and went back to sleep. When I looked out the window again, it was gone."

The TV screen switched back to the newscaster. He flashed a perfect smile.

"Strangely enough, police say there have been robots reported at the site of three other incidents. The mechanical vandals are believed to be sci-fi fans dressed in costume for the annual Mega-Monster Film Festival."

The TV guy was probably right. When I'd gone to the movie downtown, an awful lot of the weirdos hanging out there were dressed like robots—like the guy who looked like Monster and followed me into the alley. Now that I thought about it, a bunch of them looked sort of like Monster. You'd think those science-fiction fanatics would spend more time on their costumes. The ones I saw were all crummy and boxy and …

My mouth was full of Choco-Sockos and milk, but I was too stunned to swallow. Why hadn't I seen it earlier? Those weren't sci-fi fans—they were robots! My robot hadn't just multiplied in the lab—he'd multiplied at the exhibit hall! And who knew where else? There could be robots everywhere. And with the film festival going on, who'd even notice?

It was too awful to think about, but it was true! My robots were the smashers!

CHAPTER 34

The Robot Fighter

"Uncle Ben!" I gasped.

I grabbed the phone and tried to call him, but there was no answer.

"Katie Beth, will you drive me to Uncle Ben's shop?"

"Why?"

"I'm afraid he's going to be attacked by robots!"

It's hard to describe the look she gave me, except to say that it was every stupid name in the world rolled into a single stare. Katie Beth wasn't taking me anywhere.

"I'm going to a movie with Hannah. You're on your own," she said.

Oh great! The one time I had a real robot emergency and there wasn't a licensed driver in sight. Since I had no other choice, I jumped on my bike and pedaled my way toward the Electro-A-Go-Go. I knew if I cut across the dark, snowy, snake-infested field where I'm pretty sure I saw a coyote once, I could save a good five minutes. I don't know if I would've done it for anyone else, but I did it for my uncle Ben.

I could feel twigs and stumps touching my legs as I tore across the field. Every shadow looked like a savage creature ready to pounce. It was getting dark, but I could've sworn I saw a mass migration of something moving through the evergreens—possibly a herd of deer or gorillas. But the worst part was the pine branches that seemed to reach out and slap me in the face. It was like long green arms were trying to grab me! My mind flashed back to that movie Dad was watching, the one with the giant man-eating plant.

"Feed me!" it had said.

And just like that, a thought wriggled into my brain and sat down. Feed me? Could it be that simple?

Feed me! Of course, that was it! That's why the robots were smashing things. They were draining the batteries! They were feeding on the power! And when they'd eaten their fill, they multiplied! Just like the plant in the movie! I pedaled faster and felt the bump under my wheels as I jumped the snow-covered curb at the end of the field.

Finally, I pulled up in front of my uncle's store and squealed the brakes. The front of the building was dark and empty-looking. I tried the door—it was unlocked!

When I stepped inside, I heard a terrible crashing noise coming from the back.

"Uncle Ben!" I yelled.

CRASH!

"Don't worry, Howard!" he called back. "I've got this completely under control!"

I rushed through the swinging door that led to the back of the shop. The place was a wreck. Tables were turned over and stuff was all over the floor. In the corner, I spotted Uncle Ben. He had a robot in a headlock and was punching it in its cardboard face. Another robot was trying to get past him, but Uncle Ben kept it back by kicking wildly whenever it got too close.

"Hey, buddy!" he said brightly. "What are you doing here? I thought you had your Winter Formal tonight."

The robot under his arm tried to squirm away, and Uncle Ben rammed its head into a cabinet door.

"You go on, now, Howard. Have fun!" he said. "I've just got a couple of things to finish up here."

I raced around the storeroom looking for something— anything!—I could use as a weapon. After a second, I spied a yellow-colored board in the corner and picked it up. Then I moved in on the attacking robot.

WHAP!

I bashed the big square torso so hard that the board snapped in half. The robot stumbled forward but showed no sign of lasting damage. In desperation, I leaped on its back and tried to sink my teeth into its thick, brown skull. It whirled like a rodeo bull and tossed me off.

When I looked up, the robot was headed straight at me. It raised its arm into smashing position, but paused in mid-reach. Then it did something I never expected—it fell over on its side.

Uncle Ben was stunned.

"How did you do that?"

"I don't know!" I said. "I didn't even make a dent in it!"

Just then, the robot occupying my uncle's armpit swung its metal hand upward, hitting him in the head. Uncle Ben looked dazed and I ran to help, wrestling down the snake-like arm. But it was like trying to hold on to a fire hose, and when I lost my grip I was hurled back, through the swinging door that led to the front of the shop.

I lay there on the ground, battered but not broken, and, after a minute, Uncle Ben rushed in to help me.

"Are you OK?" he said, lifting me to my feet.

"What happened to the robot?" I said.

"It headed out the back door, just like the others. I was brawling with all ten of them for a while."

Ten? There were ten now?

Then I saw that Uncle Ben had a deep gash in his forehead.

"You're hurt!" I said.

"It's nothing. War wound. I made the mistake of getting in the way when they were trying to get at my electronics."

"They were feeding," I told him. "Anything electric, they smash wide open."

He nodded.

"Yeah, I figured that out about halfway through the fight. They knocked the lights out and broke just about everything in the place. But not my Apple–1. They'd have had to get through me to make it to that!"

The Apple–1 is an old-timey, collectible computer, and, if it were possible, my uncle would marry it tomorrow.

That's what he was fighting so hard to protect from the last two robots.

We walked through the swinging door, and I reached down and put my hand on the fallen robot's back. It felt like cardboard again—plain, ordinary cardboard. I opened the box.

The goo was gone!

Suddenly, a memory raced through my mind. It was something Mr. Z said in class.

"Everything eats, Howard. It's just that instead of a cheeseburger, a robot eats electricity. And, if he doesn't get it, he starves just like you and me."

The robot starved! I realized the goo must be like gas in the tank of a car. Without electricity, it couldn't expand and—finally—it ran out.

All that was left was an empty, ordinary cardboard box.

"I'm sorry, Howard," Uncle Ben said. "I couldn't stop them. And now I don't even know where to start looking. Howard? Howard?"

My mind was somewhere else. I walked back through the swinging door and looked out the large front window. I could see downtown from here. It was all lit up and shining bright for the Mega-Monster Film Festival.

To a hungry robot, it must've looked delicious.

"I know where they're going," I said.

CHAPTER
35

Mega-Monster Madness

The tires on Uncle Ben's truck squealed to a stop, and we stepped out into the strangest disaster zone you can possibly imagine. For a minute, we were too stunned to move. We just stood there taking in the bizarre scene.

"What is this?" Uncle Ben said.

I shook my head. "I have no idea."

I'm not sure anyone did. There were aliens fighting robots, and mutants fighting people dressed like robots, and people dressed like robots fighting each other. Meanwhile, vampires and werewolves and mummies brawled like monsters in the street. It was as if all the creatures in the Mega-Monster

Film Festival had suddenly jumped off the screen and started rioting.

"This is insane," I gasped. "What are we going to do?"

"You wait here and keep an eye on things. Don't go down there, you hear me? Just stay where you are and see where they go," Uncle Ben said. "I've got a plan."

He hopped back into his truck and sped away.

Now, I knew Uncle Ben had told me not to go down to where the fight was taking place, but how could I not? This was all my fault! I couldn't just stand there doing nothing. So I waded into the battle.

Once I reached the crowd, all I could see was a bunch of odd figures pushing and fighting and yelling. Some of those figures looked like robots, and some of the robots looked like Monster, but a lot of them didn't. I saw barrels with legs, and wooden crates with arms, and shiny metal people who could've been giant wind-up toys. Who knew what was underneath? Who knew what was real?

Then, about twenty-one feet away, I spied my first target. It was tall and silver with a funnel for a hat. My internal robo-radar was going crazy! Fortunately, the invader was locked in a wrestling match with Count Dracula at the moment, which made it the perfect time for a sneak attack. Carefully, I closed the gap and prepared to fling myself onto the mechanical beast. But at the last second, I stopped.

"Hey, are you a robot?" I said.

"Of course not!" it shouted. "I'm the Tin Man from *The Wizard of Oz!*"

"*The Wizard of Oz* is not a monster movie!" Dracula screamed.

Then he punched the Tin Man in the stomach.

That's when it dawned on me that these two were not fighting about my robots. In fact, a lot of the people who were fighting didn't even seem to know there *were* any robots. But I knew. I knew because I could see one of them headed straight for a lighted movie sign.

This time, I was sure. Except for his hands, which were claws, he looked almost exactly like Monster. I blazed toward him at top speed, but my path was blocked when a chubby alien hunter ran in front of me.

"Take my picture!" he yelled.

"What?" I said.

He tossed me his cell phone.

"Cheeeeeese!" he said, and put his arm around the robot.

I snapped the photo. What else could I do? The man took his phone back and ran off laughing like he was having the time of his life.

Sci-fi people are weird.

I guess I shouldn't have watched the man for as long as I did, because that's when the robot hit me. I felt his goo-filled arm bash against my chest, launching me against the side of the brick building. Now, instead of heading for the sign, he was headed for me. I was trapped! I looked for a weapon, but it was too late. The robot was coming closer, and I saw him raise up a terrifying metal pincher. I held my hands in front of my face and waited to be squashed like a skinny grape. But just then, a quick, hairy blur sailed in front of me.

BAM!

The collision was ground-shaking. A figure in a Wolfman mask had thrown a flying body block on the attacking robot, sending it crashing against the pavement. The wolf sprung up and put its foot on the robot's back.

"Hey robo-dork!" the Wolfman said. "Keep your claws off my little brother!"

It was Stick! Stick, my tormentor-in-chief, had come to my rescue! I was speechless—but not for long.

"Watch out!" I yelled.

Two more robots suddenly appeared. Stick wheeled around, but they were already right behind him, and then ...

WHAP!

One of the robots punched the other. He socked him hard in the side of his boxy skull, and the unsuspecting goo-man staggered. Without saying a word, Stick fell onto all fours behind the stumbling robot's legs.

"Now!" he said.

The puncher kicked the woozy robot in the gut, sending it over Stick's back and onto the ground.

I was confused. That confusion turned into panic when I saw the standing robot do exactly what I'd been dreading—he pulled his head off! But instead of a squishy, multiplying ooze, I saw my dad's face.

"You guys OK?" he asked.

I nodded.

"Howard, you shouldn't be here," Dad said. "Something very strange is going on."

"Fun, though," Stick said.

"Dad, there's something you should know," I said. "About these robots, I …"

I didn't get the chance to finish my confession. A super-bright light shined into my eyes, and I winced and covered my face.

"Howard!" Uncle Ben shouted. "Come on!"

"That's Uncle Ben," I said. "I'll go with him."

Dad looked around. The police had arrived and were breaking up fights, but the battle was still raging.

"Your sister and Hannah are out here somewhere," he said. "As soon as we find them, we'll head for home. In the meantime, you stay with Ben."

Dad winked at Stick, and then they both picked up metal trash can lids, which they held like shields. I had a sneaky suspicion they weren't finished robot hunting.

Turning around, I ran to Uncle Ben's truck. When I got there, I saw that he'd loaded a large portable spotlight in the back.

"It took me a while to find one of these," he said, tapping the mega-bright light. "If we're lucky, we can use it as bait."

187

Of course! The robots were hungry for power—that's why they'd headed for the lights of downtown. So, to lure them away, we needed to show them a brighter light. My uncle was a genius! I climbed into the back of the truck.

"I'm going to drive down the street. When you see anything that looks like a robot, hit it with the light," he said.

We cruised past the theater, and I shined the giant beacon into the crowd. Sure enough, the robots began to emerge. We kept moving, and I shot the light beam down every street and into every dark alley. Before long, we were being followed by a lengthy chain of robots. They marched behind us like electric zombies looking to feed.

It was working! The robots were drawn to the light. Uncle Ben drove really slowly, and there were a couple of times the metal pinchers were so close I had to duck down into the bed of the pickup to keep from getting clawed. But at least we had them away from the film festival.

We rolled steadily back toward Uncle Ben's store. But I knew we'd never make it. Something strange was happening. The robots farthest away from the truck were turning and going in another direction. We were losing them! Then the robots in front turned too—and that's when I saw it. A huge, powerful beam of light was piercing the night sky like a knife. It was a searchlight, the kind they use at grand openings and football games … and it was … coming from the school!

"Uncle Ben!" I screamed. "They're headed for the Winter Formal!"

CHAPTER 36

Crashing the Formal

I jumped into the cab of the pickup, and we raced toward Dolley Madison. Uncle Ben's head was still bleeding, so I found a box of tissues in the truck and handed him some. He held them against the wound ... I just held my stomach. Like the rest of me, it felt miserable.

"I'm sorry, Uncle Ben," I said.

He nodded.

"I'm sorry too, squirt," he said, and he peeked at me out of the corners of his eyes. "I'm sorry for the guys in my video-game club. Because while they're sitting at home pushing buttons on a plastic controller, I'm out here fighting robots. How cool is that?"

He winked at me. All of a sudden I realized I had absolutely no reason to apologize to my uncle. It's like his whole movie-watching, game-playing life had been leading up to this moment.

We pulled up in front of the gym and sprinted to the door. A spiffy-looking version of Josh Gutierrez met us outside.

"You can't go in dressed like that," he told me. "It's a formal!"

I looked down. I was still wearing red sneakers, jeans, and a T-shirt that said "Laboratory Animal." Worse, my handkerchief didn't match any of them.

"This is an emergency!" I said, and pressed forward.

Josh put his hand up. "Crystal said to keep out anybody who's wearing jeans. So why don't you just go back to where …"

He swallowed the end of the sentence. Something in the distance had caught his attention, and his face turned as white as the fancy pressed shirt under his suit coat. I knew what he was looking at. Robots—rows and rows of them—were coming over the big hill behind the school.

We all gulped.

"Well," Uncle Ben said, "at least they're not wearing jeans."

"I'm going in!" I yelled, dashing through the door.

This time, Josh didn't stop me. I ran inside the building and almost crashed into Mr. Z, who was one of the chaperones.

"Howard?" he called.

"No time, Mr. Z!" I said, and blew past him.

I'd barely made it onto the brown hardwood floor when Kyle Stanford moved into my path. He hunkered down in a linebacker's stance, but I dropped to my knees and slid between his legs. Scrambling to my feet, I headed into a crowd of dancers.

"Stop!" I yelled. "Listen to me!"

It was no use. My voice was squashed by the heavy music. Then, just as I was about to go for the super-scream, Joni Jackson's boogieing hips launched me into Skyler Pritchard, who careened me into Dino Lincoln, and before I knew it I was bouncing around the floor like I was in a pinball machine. When the ricocheting stopped, I tilted back my head to belt out a warning. Unfortunately, that was the exact moment when the disco ball unleashed a thousand tiny death beams, temporarily frying my retinas. As the world slowly came back into view, my eyes fell on the streamers and bows and balloons hanging like decorative cobwebs from the walls and ceiling. They looked nice. Now that I thought about it, so did my classmates. I started to feel all weird and smiley inside, and that's when I realized something.

This was how prombies felt all the time!

I shook my head until the dreamy, dazed feeling left, then worked my way to the front of the gym. Time was running out. Frantically, I waved my arms to get the deejay's attention.

"Stop the music!" I screamed. "Stop the music!"

To my enormous surprise, it stopped. Now every eye was on me.

"We need to evacuate this building!" I yelled. "There's no time to explain, they'll be here any—"

SMASH!

The robots must have reached the searchlights.

An eerie silence took over the gym. I looked at the stunned faces staring back at me—and then I saw her.

Winnie McKinney was standing by the punch bowl. She was wearing a pretty pink dress, and her hair had little white flowers in it. You'd think flowers in a girl's hair would look stupid, like her head was full of dirt or something. But it was actually really cool. I thought about what she'd said, about wanting to make a memory. I was pretty sure this wasn't the one she had in mind.

"Oh, Howard," she said, her face filled with horror. "What did you do?"

CRASH!

They were here.

I watched Mr. Z try to block the door, but the stream of goo-filled party crashers knocked him to the ground. Instantly, the room exploded into screams and panic. The robots paid no attention, but quickly went to work smashing lights and feeding on the sweet, electric nectar. Suddenly, Kyle Stanford burst out of the crowd and grabbed one of the attackers from behind. He was joined by Josh Gutierrez, who began pounding the robot's gut like a cardboard punching bag. The box bent but it did not break, and the three of them tangled up like well-dressed wrestlers.

The Battle of Dolley Madison had begun!

On the far side of the gym, I saw Winnie McKinney and Missi Kilpatrick crouched behind the overturned refreshment table. When they emerged, they bombed the robots with cookies and cake and a variety of purple-tinged eating utensils. Gerald Forster rushed one of the creatures, but it dodged him like a matador, and he went sprawling across the floor. I started to help, but a brilliant flash of pink caught my eye. It was Crystal Arrington's beloved iPhone. A skinny, bucket-headed robot was holding it in the air like a trophy ... not a smart move.

CLANK!

The hit was brutal. A metal folding chair slammed against the bucket, and the robot dropped like an anchor. Crystal bent over and took the pink prize from its claw.

"Never ... touch ... my ... phone!" she screamed.

Crystal had won her fight—others weren't so lucky. The bigger, stronger robots were flinging kids aside like helpless ragdolls. I had to do something! But what?

"RRRRREEEEEEEEEE!"

An ear-bursting noise shot from the speakers. The deejay, while trying to crawl for the exit, had accidentally bumped into his keyboard and triggered a short, musical blast. Every kid in the place winced.

But every robot froze.

For a second, I was confused ... What just happened?

Then a small, banana-shaped memory danced through my brain.

"Do that again!" I yelled to the deejay. "Play something!"

It was no use. The man shook his head and ran for the nearest door. Almost instantly, the robots resumed their attack. I crawled for the keyboard, but a pair of legs cut me off.

"I've got this, Howard," Trevor said.

Trevor! I never expected to see him at the Winter Formal. He didn't seem like the type. Then again, neither did I. But here we both were, mixing it up with the popular kids and the robots. Who would've believed it?

Trevor loosened his tie and touched a black key. A long, true note echoed through the gym. Then he wheeled to his right, flipping switches and twisting knobs like an expert technician. Music blasted through the speakers. He pumped up the bass and added a beat, and that's when everything changed. The robots stopped smashing things and moved as a pack to the middle of the gym. It was like some sleeping part of them was waking up, and they were trying to shake off the grogginess. After a few seconds, one of them started to vibrate and bounce. Another one began to twitch all over. But most of them just stood there. To me, it seemed like they were confused and waiting for input. What kind of input, I had no clue.

I mean, I knew that somewhere inside of them was a tiny technology that used to make a boogie-banana dance, but how could I activate it? My thoughts wandered back to that first day with Monster when I walked around the room and he followed me. He even followed me through the lab tunnel. And that's when an unimaginably unwelcome thought crept into my skull.

"No!" I told myself. There had to be another way.

But a few of the robots had already wandered back to their old activities, and the rest looked antsy. I sighed. My task was clear. Trevor was playing the music, but someone was going to have to show them what to do with it.

It was the moment I'd dreaded since I first heard the words "Winter Formal." I closed my eyes and marched out to the front of the robot herd. Next stop, the bottom of the Dolley Madison Middle School popularity ladder.

"Crank it up," I told Trevor.

He did. The music pounded like a pulsating, super-sized drum. My body could feel the beat pouring out of the speakers.

"All right, robots!" I yelled. "Follow me!"

I held out my arms and started to spin.

The robots did the same.

I swayed to the left.

They swayed to the left.

I swayed to the right.

They swayed to the right.

Then I busted out one of my patented steps, the one that made me look like a deranged orangutan. The robots did it too—only, somehow, they made it look cool.

I kicked. I twirled. I shimmied, and my arms and legs flopped around as if the bolts that held them in place had sprung loose. The faces that remained inside the gym peeked out of their hiding places. They looked bewildered. Whether it was because of the robots or my dance moves, I'll never know.

All that mattered was that the robots had stopped smashing things. It was working! But I was getting tired. Then the oddest thing happened. Winnie McKinney crawled from behind the refreshment table and walked onto the dance floor. She started dancing with the robots! Then Wendell Mullins did the same thing. And before I knew it, Crystal was out there. Then Kyle and Missi and Josh and Dino. Finally, I saw Mr. Z and Uncle Ben walk out and stand between the robots.

I couldn't believe it. My uncle Ben was dancing!

They were all out there following my moves, pushing the robots to keep going. It was amazing. And then, just like that, one of the robots fell over on his side. It was exactly the way it had happened at Uncle Ben's store. It was out of juice. Then another one fell, and another, and another. The dance was draining their power, and the robots were dropping like large, clumsy flies.

Finally, the last of the boogie-bots fell and the invasion was over. I looked out at the rows of vacant cardboard and collapsed. I was exhausted. When the music stopped, I heard the sounds of police sirens closing in.

I opened my eyes and saw Mr. Z standing over me. His face was full of questions.

"Howard," he said, "what just happened here?"

I was going to answer. I was going to tell him everything and let the punishments fall down on me like rain.

But something else had caught my attention. Looking out through the gym door, I saw a shape on the hill overlooking the school. It was a small silhouette against the full moon, but it was as familiar to me as the back of my hand.

It was Monster.

Uncle Ben followed my eyes and came to the same terrible conclusion. There was one more robot out there that had to be stopped before there were more.

"Go," he told me.

Without another word, I dashed out the front door and across the parking lot. My lungs ached when I hit the hill, but I kept moving. If Monster got away and replicated, everything we'd done tonight would have been for nothing. It would all start over again.

CHAPTER 37

The Chase

I knew it was Monster. The minute I saw the figure on the hill, I just knew.

"He looks evil," Franklin had said.

I hadn't seen it then. But I saw it now.

I reached the top of the hill and started across the dark, creepy field. It was the same one I'd had to cross to get to Uncle Ben's store. I was almost hoping a cold, robotic hand would reach out and grab me—at least then I'd know where he was. At the moment, he was just another unseen horror in the shadows.

But he didn't stay unseen for long. I rounded a group of pine trees, and there he was, the full moon making him look extra-large

and extra-menacing. He wasn't even trying to get away. It was like he was, I don't know, waiting for me.

"Take it easy," I told him. "We'll go back to the lab and work this out."

Monster stared at me. Of course, since robots can't blink, staring was pretty much his only option. Still, something about the way he did it was blood-chilling. And then questions ran through my mind: What if he wanted me to follow him here? Could this be a trap? It was an awful thought, and I tried to push it out of my head. But an instant later, I saw something moving in the pine trees.

Monster wasn't alone.

There was another robot! Through the pine brush, I could see the moonlight glistening off its cruel, mechanical arms. It was headed right for us! If it got behind me, I'd be trapped with no hope of escape. I wanted to turn on my heels and run—but didn't. For some reason, I stood my ground. I didn't know why—there was just something about that second robot. He looked so … familiar.

"Mr. Jolly?" I said.

It was! It was Mr. Jolly! It was my big, happy, metal-armed, motorized snowman! He was rolling through the trees and making a beeline for Monster. How was this possible? I watched as he hit the robot and sent him stumbling against a tree trunk. Monster recovered and took a hard swing at the snowman, almost toppling him over. But Mr. Jolly kept his balance and responded with a big, metal-fisted punch of his own.

I stared in amazement as the two warriors matched

each other in ferocious robo-combat. Finally, the snowman moved in and wrapped his huge arms tightly around his mechanical opponent. My mouth dropped open—Mr. Jolly was hugging Monster!

And not just any hug—an inescapable hug of robotic steel!

"I've got him, Howard!" a voice yelled. "I've got him!"

Wait a minute. I knew that voice. It was Franklin! Franklin's voice was coming from Mr. Jolly! Was he controlling the snowman? I moved in closer and saw that in the place where Mr. Jolly's face should have been, there was a tablet computer. And there on the screen, with a monster-sized smile, was the big, hairy, wonderful face of my very best friend in the world.

"You're safe now, Howard," Franklin said. "I won't let go. I won't let go for anything."

He didn't. The robot struggled for a while, but after a few minutes, his power was gone. I watched his fierceness leave, and all that remained was a harmless stack of cardboard.

While I wouldn't fully understand what happened until later, I did know this: the robots were finished, and Franklin had saved me. That might have been the end of the story. But there was a little bit more to do.

Return to Snowblind Alley

It was a calm, sunny Saturday morning. The smell of pine needles and chimney smoke hovered on the wind. In the distance, a short, well-dressed figure glided smoothly down the street, his black suit making him look like a grinning penguin in a snowy, white world.

When Butler-bot had reached the exact center of Snowblind Alley, he stopped, turned his head, and waited.

And waited.

And waited. After several tension-filled minutes, Kyle Stanford emerged from his hidden bunker on the north side of the street. Carefully, he approached the robot and picked up the clown-shaped walkie-talkie on the serving tray. The mechanical butler rotated its head until it appeared to be staring him directly in the face. Then it winked.

Kyle put the walkie-talkie to his ear.

"Hello?" he said.

"Hello, Kyle," I answered through the clown's mouth. "This is Howard Boward."

For the longest time, no words came out of my speaker. But I'm pretty sure the clown growled at me.

Now, if you're wondering why I was talking to Kyle on a walkie-talkie in the first place, it's because that seemed like the best way to communicate without having to be anywhere near him. I mean, the last time I was on Snowblind Alley, I got hit with several dozen snowballs before I could even open my mouth.

As for why the walkie-talkies looked like circus clowns, well, they were Orson's. Since my entire plan depended on Kyle Stanford being able to operate this piece of equipment, I figured something made for a five-year-old ought to be just about right.

I pushed the red button on the clown's enormous nose.

"Listen, things have gotten a little out of hand lately," I said, "and I was wondering if we could have a meeting."

"Sure," Kyle said. "We can have a meeting between my fist and your face."

"Funny you should say that, because that's just the kind of thing I want to talk about," I told him. "You know, the beatings, the snowballs, the swirlees, sticking someone's tongue to a metal pole and leaving them there ..."

A loud, ugly laugh burst from the speaker. That's when I realized that, for Kyle, these weren't criticisms—they were a list of his greatest hits. I took a deep breath and continued.

"Anyway, I was thinking maybe we could just start fresh. You know, you forget that I make good grades, and I'll forget that you make me wear my underpants like a hat."

I heard a snort on the other end of the clown.

"Why would I want to do that?"

"I'm glad you asked," I said, and nodded to Gerald Forster.

On cue, Gerald picked up his remote control and steered Basket-bot out onto Mulberry Street. A few seconds later, Richard Patel did the same thing with Putt-Putt, and the other BAs weren't far behind. Within a minute, a small army of robots had gathered in front of the Snowblind Alley gang.

I wasn't there, of course. My group and I were set up a block away, and I watched the operation unfold through a pair of my dad's binoculars. From what I could see, it looked like the Snowblinders were curious about the robots—just not curious enough to go anywhere near them.

"Let's move," I said.

We did. And for the first time since that cold-and-horrible attack, I found myself walking down Snowblind Alley. Only this time, I wasn't alone. Gerald and the BAs, Reynolds, Wendell, and Trevor were all right behind me.

The most surprising thing was that no one tried to stop us. For a second, Mulberry actually felt like any other street—like it was open and accessible to everyone. Of course, I knew better. We all did. The only reason we'd made it this far was that the Snowblinders are easily confused. Moving as a group, we marched out to the middle of the street and stopped. They stared. We stared. But nothing happened.

It was too good to last. Out of the corner of my eye, I spotted it—a big, round, slushy snowball headed straight for me. Fortunately, Gerald saw it too. He pushed a small silver rod on his control box and, instantly, Basket-bot's robotic, hoops-shooting arm sprung upward. It blocked the projectile like a shield.

Both sides of Mulberry Street gasped.

"That was awesome!" Josh Gutierrez yelled.

He was right—it was awesome. Just not awesome enough to win over Kyle.

"Are you insane, Boward?" he yelled. "What are you doing on my street?"

I smiled and glanced at Trevor.

"We're here to teach you a lesson," I said.

That's when Basket-bot sprang into action. He rolled toward a group of Snowblinders, sending them diving for cover. With his remote control, Gerald steered the robot down the frozen sidewalk, lowering its scoop so that it picked up a massive amount of ice and snow. When it was fully loaded, it turned, faced the fleeing attackers … and dumped its bucket onto the ground.

The Snowblinders looked more confused than ever.

"Any of you guys have to shovel snow out of your driveway?" I asked.

No one answered. They didn't have to—sooner or later, just about every kid around here ends up on the business end of a snow shovel. It's a universal rite of childhood misery.

"As you've just seen, a robot can do the job in five minutes—and you never even have to break a sweat. We've got robots here that can wash windows, clean gutters, walk dogs—in fact, they can do just about any job a kid can get stuck with."

Now the Snowblinders were interested. I could tell because they finally emerged from their frosty forts and moved in for a closer look. Bulldog Busby seemed particularly fascinated by Putt-Putt—probably because it was wielding a club.

"So what are you saying, How-weird ... I mean, Howard?" he said. "Are you saying if we stop picking on you, we can use these things?"

Don't ask me how, but I knew that question was coming. I wiped the smile off my face and shook my head.

"No," I told him. "I'm saying you can't use them."

There was an eerie silence. If you know anything at all about bullies, you know this was not the answer they were looking for. But it was the answer I'd come here to give them.

You see, for years, I'd been handing over my lunch money to guys like Bulldog and Kyle and Josh. In fact, it was Bulldog and Kyle and Josh. After a while, you start to realize that paying someone not to beat you up is a pretty lousy trade. You just end up paying them again the next day.

As far as I was concerned, letting this crew use the robots would be just like giving them mechanical lunch money.

"We didn't bring these things to show you what you can have," I said. "We brought them to show you what you're missing."

This time, I got a reaction—a rumble moved through the crowd. It was bully thunder, a sure sign a beat-down was coming! I gulped and talked faster.

"Here's my point," I said. "I know you're not crazy about smart kids—but if smart kids can build stuff like this, why would you want to make us your enemy? I mean, people don't go out of their way to help an enemy. But they'd do just about anything for a friend."

This seemed to quiet the storm.

"You know what I think it is?" I told them. "It's middle school. It divides us into these little groups so we can judge people without getting to know them."

The truth is, I wasn't just talking about the bullies—I was talking about me. My eyes automatically found Trevor and Gerald.

"All I'm saying is that if we stopped thinking of each other as UPs and jocks and nerds and geeks, and just thought of each other as kids, things might be better for everybody."

The street was so quiet I thought someone must have pushed a mute button. Then a slow, sad clapping sound came from the back of the group. I didn't need to look to know it was Kyle.

"Spoken like a true nerd," he said. "And I don't hang out with nerds—I pound 'em!"

I wish I could say that surprised me, but it didn't. Kyle Stanford has a stubborn streak a mile wide. He clenched his fist and moved toward me.

"You're making a mistake," I told him.

"Really?" he said, shoving me to the ground.

I looked up at him, then glanced down the street.

"Really," I said.

The word had barely left my tongue when a snow-white, four-wheeled figure roared down the block. Franklin raced past us and did a power slide on the icy pavement. He followed it with a series of doughnuts that ran together until he was spinning like a top in the middle of the road.

Then he raised the long, plastic tube attached to Mr. Jolly's arm and fired three round, perfect ice balls into the sky.

In case you're wondering, the ice-ball shooter was new. We added it especially for this occasion, and personally, I thought it turned out pretty nice. The second the Snowblinders saw it, they scattered like frightened rabbits.

I stood up, dusted off my parka, and walked to Franklin.

"One, please," I said.

Franklin pulled a paper cone from a dispenser on his plastic belly and filled it with a perfect ice ball from the shooter. Then he turned around, revealing a tank containing three flavors of syrup—strawberry, grape, and tutti frutti.

I pulled the handle marked "tutti frutti" then sunk my teeth into the red, sugary slush.

"Who wants a snow cone?" Franklin shouted.

Almost instantly, he was surrounded by Snowblinders and UPs and BAs and Pipkins, all of them brought together by a shared love of free junk food.

What did this mean? It meant for a day—just one day—things were different. And if it could happen in Snowblind Alley, then who knows? Maybe it could happen anywhere.

All of a sudden, I was glad we didn't go with my original plan: turning the robots into an incredible, bully-seeking attack squad. I've got to admit, it was tempting—the idea of using our brains against their muscles. What stopped me was something Mr. Z had said—Believer Achievers try to treat others the way they want to be treated.

So as much as I wanted to treat the Snowblinders to some good, old-fashioned robot revenge, the real question was what I would want for myself—war or a snow cone?

I took another satisfying bite of tutti frutti. When I looked up, I almost choked on it.

Josh Gutierrez was standing in front of Franklin, staring into his tablet-sized face. The last time they'd been that close together, Franklin had his own body—and they hadn't parted on real good terms.

Josh's eyes narrowed into tiny squints. I held my breath.

"Can you make mine a double-decker?" he said.

Franklin smiled.

"Sure. Just a second."

He lifted his snow-botic arm and fired an ice ball through the middle of the crowd.

"Sorry. The tube was clogged," he said.

And it probably was. You know how unreliable technology can be. Of course, since the ice ball ended up smacking Kyle Stanford square in the stomach, I guess I can see how some people might have their doubts.

CHAPTER 39

Second Chances

There are a few loose ends you're probably wondering about. I'll try to tie them up for you.

First, the day after the Winter Formal, I helped Orson build a snowman in the front yard. It was made completely of snow and had a black hat and a corn-cob pipe and a carrot for a nose ... and glowing red eyes, and metal pinchers, and vampire teeth. My mom is praying for a heat wave.

Now, about Mr. Jolly. Reynolds found him. I guess that isn't really a surprise because, well, Reynolds finds everything. He's the biggest snoop in town. But he's also got one of the biggest brains, which is something I don't give him enough credit for.

You see, Reynolds figured out that Mr. Jolly had a problem—he couldn't think. And because he couldn't think, he just kept rolling when he should have stopped. Franklin, on the other hand, was a great thinker. In fact, since he didn't have a body, thinking was about the only thing he could do. So Reynolds put them together.

I don't mean to make it sound like it was easy. I'm sure it wasn't. Fortunately, he had a lot of help.

"G-Force did most of it," Reynolds said. "He's kind of a genius with electronics."

Actually, he kind of is. But it wasn't just Gerald; it was all the BAs. They teamed up and worked on Mr. Jolly, partly because they felt bad about not believing me when I said I didn't wreck Putt-Putt. Now that it was all over the news, everyone naturally assumed the smashers were responsible. And they were right—they just didn't know that the smashers were robots, and Monster was their king.

So the BAs were more than happy to use what they knew about robotics to turn Mr. Jolly into a plump, plastic hugging machine. When they were done, Franklin had a Facetime connection and could see everything through the tablet's camera. What's more, he could control the snowman's actions like some kind of an onboard remote control.

And, when the robots finally went on the rampage, Franklin did what he does—he came to the rescue.

As for what happened at the Winter Formal? Well, people are still trying to figure that out. Right after I left, Mr. Z met the police in the parking lot and led them into the gym. But all they found were some empty boxes, a few barrels, and other pieces of poorly made robot costumes. They called them "costumes," because what other explanation could there be? I mean, cardboard boxes don't just get up and dance all by themselves!

It was a mystery, all right. Even Mr. Z was stumped. Of

course, he might have figured it out if there'd been even a trace of goo left inside the robotic remains, but there wasn't. It was gone. So the official story was that, in the confusion, the smashers had shed their robo-skins and scurried out a side door. Sure, it was strange that no one saw a group that size getting away, but there were an awful lot of kids running around that night.

Besides, you have to expect this kind of thing during the Mega-Monster Film Festival. It attracts a lot of weirdos.

Speaking of the film festival, the riot downtown made the national news. There was a rumor that it started when someone sent real robots into the crowd. Of course, the theater owners denied it, but you know how rumors are— they die hard. Especially ones that are good for business.

They're expecting twice as many people at next year's Mega-Monster.

That leads us to Winnie McKinney. Needless to say, she was not a happy prombie. All she'd wanted was one night, just one, with everybody gathered together and the room decorated like something out of a fairy tale. I'd ruined that. It was a memory that I'd taken away forever.

I thought about that as I led her across the dirt road. She hadn't wanted to come but when I have my heart set on something, I can be very annoying.

"It's cold, Howard. Where are you taking me?"

"You'll see."

"Can I at least take off the blindfold?"

"In a second," I said.

We stepped inside the big aluminum building.

"Now," I told her.

She took off the blindfold, and there were fireworks in her eyes. I couldn't give her back the memory I took away, but her smile told me that maybe, just maybe, she'd made a new one.

Skatesville looked like, well, Skatesville. What I mean is it looked like the Skatesville I remembered from when I was a kid. Only better because it was all dressed up with the decorations from the Winter Formal.

Everybody had helped. Reynolds, Gerald, the BAs—even the UPs. They'd all pitched in and cleaned up the place. Trevor couldn't believe how many kids showed up. But it really wasn't hard to get them there. It seemed like everybody remembered Skatesville, and they all wanted to see the place come back to life.

Gerald and Richard even got the old sign on the roof working. So Skatesville officially shined again.

"Well, you're finally here!" Crystal screeched. "So are we going to skate or what?"

Winnie and I sat down and put on some skates. Then we carefully rolled onto the newly polished floor. Meanwhile, Mr. Jolly glided gracefully around us. I swear, even though the building wasn't empty anymore, Franklin's laugh echoed like he was skating through a cave. Josh, Missi, Joni, and Wendell formed a human chain and whipped past us. Dino and Kyle were ramming each other like roller derby stars. I saw Gerald skating backward ... the big show-off. Reynolds was hugging the rail.

Winnie looked at me.

"So, do I still get that dance?" she said.

I gulped. After seeing my moves with the robots, I figured dancing would be the last thing anyone would want me to do. Ever! But you never know with girls, so I'd picked out a song just in case. I nodded at Trevor, and when the music started, Winnie smiled.

We skated out to the middle of the rink, and everyone else joined us.

We put our left hands in.

We took our left hands out.

We put our left hands in, and we shook them all about.

We did the Hokey Pokey and we turned ourselves around.

Because that's what it's all about.

The End

Miss book one of the series? Then check out this excerpt from Howard's first adventure.

HOW TO MAKE FRIENDS AND MONSTERS

BY HOWARD BOWARD

WITH A LITTLE HELP FROM RON BATES

How-I-Am

You know how there's always that one kid who can't find a place to sit in the cafeteria because people "save" empty seats for imaginary friends whenever he heads their way? So he has to carry his Salisbury steak, potatoes, and hot roll all the way to the table in the very back of the room? Only he trips and falls before he gets there and, when he stands up, he's got cream gravy in his shirt pocket and green beans where his eyebrows should be?

I'm that kid.

My name is Howard Boward (yeah, thanks Mom and Dad), but most people just call me "How." Well, not just How, they call me "How Weird," or "How Lame," or "How Did You Get That Chair? It's Saved!" Things like that. Until a few weeks ago, I was more of a "Who" ("Who's the dork by the water fountain?"), a "What" ("What is wrong with that kid?") or a "Why" ("Why is he wearing a unitard?"). So, when you think about it, the fact that I am now a "How" is kind of a step up.

Not a *giant* step or anything. You can only go so far up the popularity ladder when half the seventh grade has seen you running down the hall in a unitard—which, for the record, was part of an experiment I was doing on invisibility. My hypothesis was correct: unitards cure invisibility.

I've actually created a chart of the popularity ladder and I fall somewhere between gym-class asthmatic and that dog that bit Vice Principal Hertz. It's not as bad as it sounds. A lot of people love that dog.

The point is, it's become increasingly apparent I need to improve my social status. And I need to do it fast because, in middle school, being unpopular is like having a disease. *Symptoms include fear, loneliness, wedgies, and a sudden, unexplained loss of your lunch money. If you think you may be experiencing unpopularity, ask your bully if daily beatings are right for you.*

I'm kidding! You can't ask a bully to cure a disease. Bullies are the disease! And Dolley Madison Middle School (Go Manatees!) is the center of the epidemic. I should know, I'm like candy to those people. It's weird—there's just something about me that attracts the big, brainless, and angry. I'd like to say it's my sparkling personality, but since the only thing about me that sparkles are my braces, it's probably one of these things:

Reasons I Am Bully Candy

1. I'm built for it. If they ever make a movie about those rubber stick figures that have bodies like pencils and flexible, spindly arms, Hollywood will knock at my door.

2. Somewhere behind the massive construction project in my mouth are the remains of my original teeth. I'm told I'll probably have a magnificent smile someday. I just can't imagine why I'd ever use it.

3. I have G.A.S. (Goosebumps Addictive Syndrome). I am totally addicted to the **Goosebumps** novels by R.L. Stine. I read them in the bathroom at school because, when I get to the scary parts, I tend to scream. This is a completely involuntary response. Coincidentally, pretty much the whole school thinks I have some painful digestive-disorder, though I've told them repeatedly, "No, I have G.A.S." This doesn't help.

4. I use big words like "digitibulist" when I could just say "thimble collector."

5. I am a digitibulist.

6. My hair is cotton white and stands bolt-upright on the top of my head so that I constantly look like

I've been frightened by a creature in an Abbott and Costello movie.

7. I watch Abbott and Costello movies.

8. I have "nerdism," a condition that requires me to love science and wear bulky, un-cool eyeglasses.

9. The other kids are all jealous of me. (This one is kind of a long shot but it makes the list come out with ten items. I like to list things in groups of exactly ten.)

10. I am smart.

Number 10 is the worst offense, and the one most responsible for my problem. See, your average bully can smell a big, juicy brain from up to three blocks away. That's bad news for me. Imagine roaming through a pack of wild dogs with bacon in your head.

(FYI, I don't actually know what a brain smells like. But intelligence smells like bacon.)

Now, about the "incident" ... I guess it would be easy to blame what happened in the fall of seventh grade on the bullies, but I won't. No one made me do what I did. Everything that went wrong, and all the madness that came from it, is my responsibility. Judge me as you will.

All I ask is that you keep in mind I am only twelve years old, I had a ton of homework, and these were my first monsters.